"Police!" Sheila Said To The Tall Figure In The Shower. "Don't Move!"

But he did move. He pushed the glass shower door open, saw the gun in her hand and then froze.

He was as handsome as a god. Hot water cascaded down a long back, narrow hips and well-muscled legs. He was about six-two, and a hundred and eighty well-distributed pounds. And his face was something out of the movies.

Sheila realized her mouth was open and managed to shut it. Belatedly she showed him her shield. "Police officer. Would you mind stepping out of there?"

"Yes, I would. What the hell's going on?"

"I could ask you the same question," Sheila replied coolly, tucking her shield back in her pocket and keeping her weapon steady. "You got a name?"

He eyed the revolver. "I'm Max Bollinger."

"Got any ID?"

He had a good smile. It came slowly, slipping attractively to one side of his mouth. He raised the palms of both hands to indicate his lack of pockets. "Not on me—at the moment."

Dear Reader:

Welcome! You hold in your hand a Silhouette
Desire – your ticket to a whole new world of
reading pleasure.

As you might know, we are continuing the *Man of
the Month* concept through to May 1991. In the
upcoming year look for special men created by
some of our most popular authors: Elizabeth
Lowell, Annette Broadrick, Diana Palmer, Nancy
Martin and Ann Major. We're sure you will find
these intrepid males absolutely irresistible!

But Desire is more than the *Man of the Month*.
Each and every book is a wonderful love story in
which the emotional and sensual go hand-in-hand.
A Silhouette Desire can be humorous or serious,
but it will always be satisfying.

For more details please write to:

Jane Nicholls
Silhouette Books
PO Box 236
Thornton Road
Croydon
Surrey
CR9 3RU

NANCY MARTIN

LOOKING FOR TROUBLE

Silhouette Desire

Originally Published by Silhouette Books
a division of
Harlequin Enterprises Ltd.

First published in Great Britain in 1991 by Silhouette Books, Eton House, 18-24 Paradise Road, Richmond, Surrey TW9 1SR

© Nancy Martin 1990

Silhouette, Silhouette Desire and Colophon are Trade Marks of Harlequin Enterprises B.V.

ISBN 0 373 58162 9

22 – 9105

Made and printed in Great Britain

NANCY MARTIN

has lived in a succession of small towns in Pennsylvania, though she loves to travel to find locations for romance in larger cities – in this country and abroad. Now she lives with her husband and two daughters in a house they've restored and with which they are constantly tinkering.

If Nancy's not sitting at her word processor with a stack of records on the stereo, you might find her cavorting with her children, skiing with her husband, or relaxing by the pool. She loves writing romance and has also written as Elissa Curry.

Other Silhouette Books by Nancy Martin

Silhouette Desire

Hit Man
A Living Legend
Showdown
Ready, Willing and Abel

One

On a cold, rainy March night, Detective Sheila Malone and her partner had delivered a prisoner to federal agents at the airport, and were back on the expressway heading into the city. As they drove, the radio squawked, barely audible over the thunder of sleet on the roof and the clatter of windshield wipers. Sheila leaned forward and turned up the radio in time to hear Dorothy, the dispatcher, announce that two officers needed backup pronto: burglary in progress.

"That's only a couple of blocks from here," Sheila said, when Dorothy reeled off the suburban address.

Cowboy shook his head. Greg Stankowsky was known to most of the cops at the precinct house as "Cowboy" because he had been a mounted police officer in New York City before he moved to the Midwest. "I know what you're thinking, Malone," he said. "Forget it. This isn't our jurisdiction."

"They could use our help."

"No way! You're supposed to be off active duty, and my orders were to deliver the prisoner and go straight back to the precinct. You're not even supposed to be along for the ride."

"I'm sick of paperwork." She pulled the car off the exit ramp and headed into the suburbs.

Cowboy sighed. "I'm a lousy baby-sitter."

Within minutes they saw the black-and-white of two uniformed cops parked in the driveway of a huge mansion on a tree-lined street. The car's light was flashing, plus the house was lit up like a Christmas pageant with floodlights that were hidden in the glistening shrubbery.

"What a place," said Cowboy. He pulled his gun out and checked it, then glanced across at Sheila. "Can you handle this, Malone? I mean, it's a little soon."

"I'm not a basket case," she replied, getting out of the car and leading the way to the front door with long-legged strides. She had to prove a few things—to herself as much as to the rest of the police force. Sheila Malone was no wimp.

The owner of the house was hysterical on her own front steps. She was a handsome older woman dressed as if she had just come home from an audience with the Queen—her wet fur coat hung open to reveal a long dress made out of some sparkly material, and jewelry of the sort you don't see every day. But there were two huge streaks of mascara running down from her pathetic, startled eyes which brimmed with more tears.

Sheila flashed her badge at the other cops. "What's going on?"

The two uniforms looked young and nervous. The small-boned black female officer had her arm around the hysterical lady, while her partner—a former football-player type with a baby face and fuzzy blond hair—questioned the woman.

The baby face explained: "Mrs. Pletheridge came home from the opera and discovered her back door broken in. She went upstairs and found that somebody had stolen some jewelry. While she was phoning in the 911, she heard a noise and figured the guy was still in the house."

Sheila shielded her eyes against the rain and glanced at the upstairs windows where numerous lights blazed. "Anyone else live here with you, Mrs. Pletheridge?"

Mrs. Pletheridge burst into a fresh torrent of noisy weeping. "No, no, no, it's only me now. My husband is away, my children moved out—"

"Any servants, Mrs. P.?" Cowboy asked, sounding bored—a sure sign he was as tight as a watch spring inside. "A butler? A chauffeur?"

She shook her head, wiping her elegant nose on her glove. "I c-can't afford them anymore."

"Okay," said Sheila, taking charge. She nodded at the woman cop. "Escort Mrs. Pletheridge to the car. The three of us will check the house."

Cowboy was already through the door, his gun drawn. The baby face followed and Sheila wasn't far behind. They found themselves in a huge foyer with a chandelier big enough to light a basketball court. Dripping water on the glorious Oriental rug, the three cops glanced around. Two monster-size Chinese vases flanked the front door, and the curved staircase looked ready for a Busby Berkeley dance routine.

"Let's not break anything, sports fans," Cowboy advised sotto voce.

"I'll say," breathed the anxious uniformed cop. "What is this place? Some kind of museum?"

"Shall we go upstairs, everybody?" Sheila suggested.

"Malone, you're such a romantic."

She let that one pass, glad that her partner didn't feel the need to treat her like an invalid. "I figure there're two stairways in a place like this—one for company, the other for the Irish maid."

"Probably right. You have an Irish maid in your family tree, Malone?"

"Several."

Cowboy put his hand on the newel post and started up the curved steps. "Okay, use your instinct to find the backstairs. We'll meet you on the second floor."

"What are we looking for?" the baby face asked. "You think the burglar is still in the house?"

"Sure," said Cowboy. "He's probably a clever cat burglar just back from Monte Carlo, and we're gonna get international publicity for catching him. Stay alert. These master-criminal types are experts in karate, you know."

Cowboy's joke didn't alleviate the tension. A cat burglar wasn't as likely an intruder as a doped-up punk looking for valuables to sell for his next hit. Moving silently in her sneakers, Sheila found the kitchen—a cavernous room with two stainless-steel stoves and a refrigerator that had to be an antique. She saw the broken windowpane in the back door and a puddle of rainwater on the tile floor. Beyond a swing door lay a dining room big enough to seat a class reunion. Sheila tried another door and found a second staircase. The stairwell was dark, but she could see a light at the top.

She inhaled a steadying breath and drew her revolver for the first time since Tuesday night, when all hell had broken loose. She noticed her hand was trembling. Waiting at the bottom of the steps, Sheila stared at the gun until the shaking stopped. Then she started cautiously up the stairs.

Reaching the top, she spotted Cowboy and the baby face waiting for her in the center of a T-shaped hallway. They all stood like statues with guns drawn, listening, straining to hear some small sound that would pinpoint the perpetrator. No luck.

No cop enjoys sneaking through a strange house wondering if some small-time hood is going to pop out of a closet with an assault rifle. The uniformed cop looked terrified, and Sheila wondered if her own face showed the fear she felt building inside.

Cowboy silently gestured with his empty hand, indicating that he would take the third floor himself. The baby face turned left down the hallway, so Sheila went right. Everybody tiptoed.

Halfway down her end of the hallway, Sheila heard the noise. Her heart started skipping in her chest at the sound—a rookie's reaction that she cursed. With adrenaline singing in her veins, she considered going back to get Cowboy, but in a moment of clear thinking she decided that no truly dangerous burglar was going to take a shower in the home he was ripping off.

She followed the noise of running water to a bedroom at the end of the hall. The light was on—a pretty china lamp that gave off very little illumination.

It was a nice room—four-poster bed, thick blue carpet underfoot. She swept the room with a quick glance. Some clothes had been thrown across the coverlet, and he'd left his shoes in the middle of the floor. There was a suitcase lying open on the bed, and the clothing packed in it was neatly folded. A half-empty bottle of beer stood sweating condensation onto the paperback book that lay on the dresser.

Whoever he was, he'd made himself at home.

The bathroom door was partway open and steam was billowing into the bedroom along with a blaze of fluorescent light. Sheila nudged the door open with her left hand. Her revolver was steady in her right—surprisingly steady.

"Police," she said to the tall figure in the shower, raising her voice to be heard over the thunder of the spray. "Don't move!"

Of course, he moved. He cursed first—out of surprise. Then he pushed the glass shower door open, saw the gun in her hand and froze. His gaze shot to her face, and he cursed again, prayerfully this time.

He was as handsome as a god and just as naked.

Sheila realized her mouth was gaping and managed to close it. Belatedly she showed him her shield. "Police officer. Would you mind stepping out of there?"

"Yes, I would," he said, sounding very much like an outraged Monte Carlo cat burglar. All that was missing was a hoity-toity English accent. "What's the hell's going on here?" he demanded.

Sheila mustered her cop's persona. "I could ask you that same question, Slick. What are *you* doing?"

"What does it *look* like I'm doing?"

Even dripping wet, it was easy to see that he was an astoundingly handsome man in his late thirties, though it was a little hard to calculate his age with so many other distractions to draw her eye. The hot water cascaded down his broad chest, his narrow hips and muscled legs. He was about six-two, she guessed, and a hundred eighty well-distributed pounds. He had the shoulders of a linebacker and the torso of a Greek statue. His face was like something out of the movies, with dramatic brows drawn down over dark, dangerous eyes.

"It looks like you're taking a shower," she replied coolly, tucking her badge back into her pocket and keeping her weapon steady. "You got a name?"

He eyed her revolver. "Maybe you could put the gun away before we get to the introductions?"

Sheila kept her weapon trained on the patch of black hair on his chest. She had held many a man at bay over the past six years and they reacted in a limited number of ways. There were the wise guys, the innocents and the smart ones. "I like you nervous, Slick. Tell me who you are."

He took the smart route. "I'm Max Bollinger."

"Got any ID?"

He had a good smile. It came slowly, slipping attractively to one side of his mouth. His dark eyes filled with sparkle at the same time. His face was full of charm, intelligence and calculated sex appeal. He raised the palms of both hands to indicate his lack of pockets. "Not on me at the moment."

Sheila glowered. "You have a reason for being in this house?"

"It's *my* house."

"What?"

"Well, it's my mother's house, actually, but—"

"This place belongs to Mrs. Pletheridge."

"Right. She's my mother."

"I thought your name was Bollinger."

"It is. She married Pletheridge after my father died."

"I see." Sheila relaxed inside, stepped back a pace and leaned one shoulder against the bathroom doorjamb. She kept the gun on him just in case. Judging by the growing gleam in Bollinger's eye, he didn't mind the gun. In fact, she began to wonder if he wasn't starting to *enjoy* the situation just a little bit. He very obediently did not move to cover himself, which went a long way to Sheila's enjoying the situation, too. He was easy on the eyes—but so were most good con artists. With a face and bod like his, he could get away with murder.

She pulled her brain back on track before she could make a mistake. "I get the feeling your mama wasn't expecting you tonight, Slick."

"It's Max," he corrected gently, meeting her gaze with a smile that would have melted the heart of a lesser woman.

By heaven, he *was* enjoying this! "What are you doing here, Max? Besides taking a shower, I mean?"

He put a hand on either side of the tub door and leaned there. "You mean here at the house? I just got back from a business trip."

"What kind of trip?"

"I was in Germany. My family brews Steel City Ale. We have business associates in Hamburg."

Aha. The Steel City connection helped Sheila remember why she knew the Bollinger name. The brewery was located within the boundaries of the Tenth Precinct—not to mention four blocks from Sheila's own home in the working-class South Side. She had grown up hearing the patrons of her uncle's tavern talking about their work at the brewery and their boss, Bollinger. Max looked like an aristocrat, all right. He was the owner's blue-blooded son, no doubt.

Coming back to the problem at hand, she asked, "How long have you been away, Max?"

"Four years."

"Long trip," she observed dryly.

He shrugged. "Lots of business."

"Didn't anybody tell you that you ought to let your mother know when you're coming home?"

His dark brows rose as realization began to dawn in his face. "My mother called you tonight?"

"She did, indeed. She thought you were a burglar."

With the beginnings of a sheepish grin, Max asked, "I scared her, did I?"

"Yep."

"She's always been on the nervous side." Max Bollinger's amused gaze studied Sheila. "Not like you, officer. You're pretty steady, aren't you?"

"I've seen it all," she answered lightly.

"But none as good as this in a while, hmm?"

With a laugh, Sheila tossed a fluffy white towel at him, and he caught it deftly. They were grinning at each other when Cowboy and the baby face entered the bedroom and came up behind Sheila. The baby face's eyes popped at the sight of Max Bollinger stark naked in the shower, with Sheila's revolver two yards away from his chest.

Cowboy pushed Sheila's hand down. "Malone," he said, "it's a cryin' shame you can't get a man any other way but this."

Sheila allowed him to twist the revolver from her hand. "This is Mrs. P.'s son, Max Bollinger. He made a surprise return from an extended business trip, hence the confusion."

"Hence? I like that word," said Cowboy, amused. "You pick that up in law school?"

"Expanding your vocabulary is a big part of self-improvement. You should try it."

"Who needs improvement?" Cowboy snapped open the chamber of her revolver and took a peek inside. His expression hardened. "Just as I suspected."

Sheila put out her hand. "Give it back, please."

"Why? It's not going to protect you from a mosquito without bullets, Malone."

From the shower, Bollinger demanded, "You mean that thing wasn't *loaded*?"

Sheila wrestled her gun back, avoiding her partner's stern glower. "Don't sound so disappointed, Slick."

"You were bluffing!"

"It worked, didn't it?"

Cowboy shot Sheila a fierce we'll-discuss-this-later look and turned to the man in the shower. "My partner hasn't been herself lately, Mr. Bollinger. Did she have a chance to explain tonight's situation to you?"

"We were getting to that, I think."

Cowboy found a wrapped cigar in the pocket of his raincoat and stuck it into the corner of his mouth. "You ought to phone home once in a while, Max. Your dear mother wasn't expecting you this evening."

"So I gather."

"Come on out there and we'll have a talk."

Bollinger even took the time to buff his dark hair before finally wrapping the towel around his trim hips and stepping out into the bedroom. He eyed Sheila sardonically, clearly miffed that she had snowballed him with the empty gun. The uniformed cop went downstairs to soothe Mrs. Pletheridge and to let her know the man upstairs was her son.

"Max," said Cowboy, putting out his hand to shake, "I'm Detective Stankowsky. You've already met my partner, Calamity Jane. Her real name's Detective Sheila Malone."

"It was a pleasure meeting her. Definitely better than the last time I was involved with the law."

Cowboy repeated. "Involved with the law?"

Max waved his hand nonchalantly. "I was found innocent."

"Uh-huh," responded Cowboy, obviously not sure if Bollinger was joking or serious. "Let's talk a minute, do you mind? Have a seat."

Bollinger sat in the chintz wing chair, and Cowboy eased down onto the edge of the bed. Sheila stayed on her feet in the bathroom doorway, waiting for her heart to stop slamming. Sometime during the last five minutes her pulse had gone crazy. With her gun tucked away, however, she began to feel better. Cowboy started the questions.

"What time did you get home tonight, Max?"

Max Bollinger crossed one long leg over the other. The dim bedside lamp illuminated the planes of his face, emphasizing the hard lines of his cheek, the proud jaw, the surprisingly sensual mouth that quirked in the polite, inquiring half-smile of a hospitable host. He was the picture of a worldly man—unruffled and elegant, even in a towel. "Around nine. Why do you ask?"

"Can you prove it?"

Sheila watched the man. Like most people questioned by the police, he seemed to be wondering what the questions could be leading to. He hesitated, studying Cowboy for clues to what was going on, then answered, "My flight arrived at eight-fifteen. The ticket's in my coat pocket, if you want to check."

Cowboy reached for Bollinger's leather jacket and started digging through the pockets. "You come straight home like a good boy?"

Watching Cowboy search his pockets, Bollinger said. "Yes, I did."

"Can you describe your movements since you got off the plane?"

He flashed an amused smile up at Sheila, saying, "This is starting to sound like I need an alibi."

Cowboy pulled out the ticket and looked at it, ignoring Bollinger's remark. "Can you describe what you've been doing since the plane landed?"

"Sure. I picked up my luggage, caught a cab at the airport and got here about nine."

Sheila looked at her watch and found it was nearly ten. It was possible that Bollinger was telling the truth, so far. They could check with the cab company to be sure. She asked, "What did you do when you got here? How did you get into the house, for instance?"

Bollinger looked at her again, his dark eyes narrowing while he tried to guess what was in the wind. "I have a key. I came in the back door—"

"The kitchen door, you mean?"

He nodded. "Right. I came in, found nobody was at home, so I ate a snack in the kitchen—some crackers, if that will save you the effort of cutting me open to make sure."

"That's the procedure only if you're dead," Sheila replied.

Cowboy sent her a let-me-handle-this look. "What then, Max?"

He sighed testily. "If you must know every detail, I opened a beer and came upstairs to get cleaned up. I'd had a long flight."

"Was anybody in the house when you arrived?"

"No."

"Hear anybody?"

"Not a thing. Look, maybe I could be more helpful if you'd tell me what's going on."

"Did you enter any other rooms in the house tonight?"

Impatient, he shot back, "What the hell is—"

"We just want to make sure we know which rooms you were in."

"I was in the kitchen, the back stairway, the hall and here. That's it."

For the first time, Sheila noticed Max's right hand. It was badly scratched with cuts across the knuckles that looked very recent. Wondering if he'd used the hand to punch a hole in the kitchen-door window downstairs, she asked, "What happened to your hand?"

Max looked at it automatically. "My hand?"

"Yeah, it's cut. How'd that happen?"

He cleared his throat. "Well, it's a little embarrassing. You probably won't believe me."

"Try us."

"I—uh—made friends with a woman on the plane. When we landed, she asked me to help her with her luggage. How was I to know she was trying to smuggle her cat into the country? She wanted to avoid the quarantine period, you see. Anyway, the cat got out, and when I tried to catch it, the damn thing attacked me." He studied the wounds. "Vicious little monsters, aren't they? I'm not fond of cats."

"Do you remember her name?"

"Foo-Foo, I think."

"The woman's name," Sheila said.

"Oh! Brenda something. I didn't plan on looking her up, you see, so I didn't catch her last name. She was just a diversion on the plane."

Sheila looked at Cowboy as if to say "Pretty feeble story."

Cowboy shrugged, then waved the airline ticket. "Mind if I keep this, Max?"

"Keep anything you like, just tell me—"

"Let's change gears for a minute," Cowboy said, glancing at the open suitcase on the bed, then eyeing Bollinger. "Where does your mother keep her jewelry?"

Bollinger looked blank. "What?"

"Do you know where your mama keeps her sparkly stuff?"

"In her bedroom, I suppose." Watching Cowboy reach toward his suitcase, Bollinger snapped, "Will someone please come to the point? I'd be much more useful if you'd—"

"When was the last time you were in your mother's bedroom?" Cowboy asked, apparently thinking twice before he rifled the suspect's suitcase without a proper search warrant. "Can you remember, Max?"

"Four years ago, at least! For God's sake, has something been stolen? Is that what this is about? Is my mother all right?" A thought hit him, and he started to get up. "My God, is she hurt?"

"Your old lady's fine," Cowboy assured him, giving Bollinger a push on his chest to send him back into the chair. "She says there's some jewelry missing."

"What jewelry?"

Mrs. Pletheridge rushed into the bedroom at that moment, her fur coat flying out behind. She was no longer crying, but her eyes were ringed with blotchy mascara, and the rest of her ruined makeup enhanced the raccoon effect. Breathing hard, she halted in the doorway, one gloved hand dramatically clutching her throat. "Max!" she cried hoarsely.

"Mother!"

Max Bollinger hadn't seen his mother in over four years. She hadn't changed in that time—same old melodramatics—but Max felt a surprising rush of affection for the dotty old dame. He had never been particularly close to her since her remarriage—nor even since the days of having a nanny around to take care of him, if the truth be known, so it wasn't so odd that Max found himself feeling like the parent as he greeted his flighty mother. "Darling, how are you?"

But Cowboy stood and moved between mother and son to block any kind of physical reunion.

With her eyes widening, Angela Pletheridge gasped, "Max, where are your clothes? What have they done to you?"

"Nothing, Mother. I just—"

"He's my son!" she cried, wheeling on Detective Stankowsky. "There's no need to strip search my own son!"

"Mother," Max began, "don't be foolish. I was taking a shower and this lovely young lady interrupted, that's all. It was almost pleasant, as a matter of fact."

Breathing raggedly, the woman glared at Detective Malone. "What are you *doing* to him?" she demanded, her voice climbing higher. "What's going on? Max, what you have *told* them? Dear heaven! *Why are you here tonight, of all nights?*"

To punctuate her statement she promptly fainted. Like a movie queen, she lifted her wrist to her brow and began to crumple slowly, giving Cowboy plenty of time to catch her in his arms. He eased her to the floor, cussing colorfully.

Unaffected by the scene he'd witnessed dozens of times in his life, Max said calmly to Detective Malone, "She does this all the time."

"Should we call the paramedics?"

"There's no need for that."

"Just make her comfortable," she said to Stankowsky.

Beside her, Max said, "I could give her this towel for a pillow."

"Keep it," she told him wryly, stepping over his mother's limp body to lend a hand in reviving her. With a glance up at Max, she remarked, "We've had enough excitement for one night."

Detective Malone patted his mother's wrists while Stankowsky applied a cool washcloth to her temples. Watching his mother pretend to come around, Max felt more amused than concerned—and a little curious. What was the old fool up to now?

She wept upon "regaining consciousness," and asked to be carried to her bedroom. The two detectives managed to wrestle the stately woman down the hall and into her room. Max didn't follow, but seized the opportunity to put on some clothes. The big old house was damned chilly and Max had been feeling more and more like an idiot wearing nothing but a towel, no matter how attractive female police detectives were these days.

When Sheila returned to his room, she found him almost dressed. He had just pulled a bulky sweater over his head.

"Disappointed?" he asked, tugging his collar into place.

She subdued a smile by turning her mouth down at the corners. "I need to use a phone. It's time to call this in."

She was an attractive woman, he decided. Not beautiful, exactly, but a stunning example of what good American genes could produce. Seeing her standing in the doorway of the bedroom made Max's throat start to ache with pleasure. She was a tall redhead with a great body and a bold, laughing look in her eye.

She was lean and lithe, with deliciously long legs that curved from slender hips. Her narrow jeans were belted with a Western-style leather belt that looked as if it had been worn like an old friend for years. Her posture was confident—maybe even cocky. Her big-shouldered denim jacket looked easy and comfortable as did the men's-style shirt that was buttoned to her breasts to reveal a ginger-colored T-shirt underneath. Her hair was pulled back from her face with a plain clip at the side of her head so that it cascaded down over her right shoulder in a riot of gleaming curls, also the color of ginger.

That bright, luxurious hair framed a surprisingly feminine face—a creamy cameo enhanced by full, saucy lips and eyes as green as lush Irish turf. Her nose was slightly too long for perfection, her chin too stubborn. In her gaze Max read intelligence and humor; but he'd also seen a flash of something else when she'd stared him down in the shower. It had been a moment of doubt, he thought; a flicker of fear.

But as she looked at him now, he wondered if she didn't seem a little disappointed to catch him with his clothes on this time.

"Are you always so businesslike, Detective?" he asked.

"I'm your tax dollars at work, Slick. Naturally, I take my job seriously. You gonna tell me where the phone is or do I have to send out a search party?"

He stood back and indicated a bedside table with a flourish. On it stood a trim, powder-blue telephone. "Here you are. Shall I leave you alone?"

"No, I'd rather keep my eye on you."

"Am I a suspect in the break-in of my own house?"

She shrugged. "It'll look a lot better for you if your fingerprints aren't all over the place. Is there a phone in the kitchen? I need to take another look at something down there."

He bowed. "Follow me."

She obeyed, trailing him down the backstairs to the kitchen. Max saw the other cops conferring outside his mother's bedroom door.

Snapping on the kitchen light, Max laid eyes on the bits of broken glass scattered across the kitchen floor. A stiff breeze whistled through a hole in the kitchen door. "What's this?" he asked. "Did the SWAT team follow you in here?"

Detective Malone appeared to be watching his reaction closely. Judging by her suspicious expression, Max realized he shouldn't have made a joke.

"Let me make this call," she said. "Then we'll talk."

"Can I clean this up?"

"Leave it for now. Why don't you make us some coffee? Is that something you can manage?"

"Sure."

Max set about obeying her while the detective reached for the phone and punched in a number.

She connected with another cop, reciting the facts as she knew them to a man on the other end of the line who must have razzed her about straying out of her usual territory. She gave as good as she got, leaning against the wall and toying with her long hair as she talked. She hung up just as Max measured water into the expensive coffee maker.

"The guys from the Third Precinct will be here in a few minutes," she reported.

"Why?" Max flipped the switch on the machine and turned to her. "I thought you and your partner had this under control."

She shook her head, strolling to the counter and flattening her hands there. In her sneakers, she was just a couple of inches shorter than Max, a size he found very appealing.

"This neighborhood isn't our beat," she explained. "We just answered a call for officer assistance, so we've got to turn it over to your local cops."

"Damn. I had hoped we might see each other a lot over this, Detective."

She allowed a grin. "Haven't I seen plenty of you already, Mr. Bollinger?"

"Max," he corrected, rounding the counter to stand beside her. "I think we know each other well enough, considering, Sheila."

Sheila turned and leaned her backside against the counter. "You haven't seen me without my clothes, so let's just leave it at Detective Malone and stick to business."

"I have a feeling you'd be an interesting woman when you're not just sticking to business."

She shook her head in mock admiration. "The babe on the plane must have done something very wrong. You've been on the ground less than two hours and already you're trying to pick up women."

With a grin, he said, "I've been homesick. Tell me, are you the average American female now, or have I hit the jackpot so soon?"

"I'm extraordinary," she replied. "Maybe you'd better start with something a little more tame."

"I don't like tame."

"What makes you think I like you at all?"

"A guess," he shot back. "How many naked suspects have you held at gunpoint for as long as you held me?"

She grinned. "I was enjoying the view."

"Well, that's a place to start, isn't it? I like looking at you, too."

"Look, Bollinger—"

"Max."

"Mad Max," she retorted, still smiling at his bold attempt to seduce an officer of the law while she was on duty. "Take a look at this situation, will you? I'm the cop and you're the suspect. You ever hear of conflict of interest?"

"We were getting along pretty well upstairs in spite of the conflict of interest. Maybe it's trite, but I thought there was something between us."

Sheila laughed shortly. "Yeah, my gun!"

He laughed, too. "All right, what do you say we get the business over with? Then we can get on to better things."

"Okay. Tell me about the last time you were involved with the law."

Max didn't expect her to start firing questions right away—and certainly not with such a composed expression on her face. "Did I say I was involved with the law?"

"Yep. What happened? Traffic ticket? Or something a little more serious?"

"It wasn't jewelry stealing, believe me."

"What, then?"

Turning away so she couldn't read his expression in case he made a mistake, Max made a show of looking through the cupboards for coffee cups. "Oh, something my father was mixed up in. Financial trouble, to tell the truth. His way of getting out of debt wasn't exactly conventional. The police wondered if I had anything to do with it."

"Did you?"

"Not at all. My father was his own boss. I was just working for him at the time."

"What happened to him?"

"He died," Max said bluntly, intending to put an end to this vein of conversation. "Coffee's ready. Can I pour you a cup?"

"Sure."

Max set cups on the counter and poured. "Sugar? Milk?"

"Black."

Passing her the cup, Max watched her take it in her slim hands. She wore her nails short, he noted—no polish, no jewelry.

She caught him looking and took a sip from her steaming cup before saying, "What are you staring at?"

"You're not wearing a wedding ring."

"So?" she challenged, her green eyes sparking over the rim of the cup.

Max leaned on the counter next to her. "Detective, I can't help thinking you liked me better when you had the upper hand."

"What's that supposed to mean?"

"You were the boss upstairs. You seemed to think I was all right when I was naked and helpless."

She shrugged with another wry grin. "That's the nature of my work. If I lost control of a situation—well, things can go bad pretty fast."

He glanced down at her open jacket where the butt of her revolver showed through. "Especially if you're in the habit of carrying an unloaded gun."

Sheila turned away abruptly. "Tonight's a special circumstance. I didn't expect to end up here."

"Still, I can't imagine any cop bothering to carry a weapon that's useless. What's the point?"

"The point is—" Sheila checked herself before her voice rose and gave her away. "Oh, never mind. I don't expect a guy like you to understand."

"What's not to understand?"

"Can we drop this, please?"

"I merely meant—"

"I don't give a damn what you meant!"

Max let a heartbeat pass without saying a word. Detective Malone suddenly blushed and said, "It's none of your business, so butt out."

"I've managed to push the wrong button somehow, haven't I?"

She shook her head, clearly embarrassed and trying to compose herself by drinking from her coffee cup. "Something happened to me, that's all. I'm not ready to carry a gun yet."

"What happened?"

"Nothing. I—I—"

"Something go wrong?"

She laughed abruptly—with no amusement. "That's an understatement! I shot somebody."

Max whistled. "What happened?"

"What do you think happened?" she demanded. "I killed him!"

As if suddenly unable to stop herself, she blurted out, "It was in the line of duty, but—Oh, hell! I never expected it to happen the way it did. So quick—so final." She set down her cup with a clatter, spilling coffee on the counter. "It's not— Damn, I'm just trying to handle it. That's all."

"By carrying an empty gun?"

Blazingly angry then, she swung at him. "Just shut up! Leave me alone. I've already talked to *two* priests, a dozen cops, a departmental shrink plus my own father and—and heard speeches from half the city's population about life-and-death situations, snap decisions, survival and—oh, all that garbage! A conversation with a perfect stranger isn't going to help."

Tears suddenly blurred those beautiful green eyes, and she hurriedly turned away.

"Maybe you're wrong," said Max, touching her arm. He couldn't prevent himself. He slid his hand up under her elbow and made a firm contact. "Maybe I can help a lot."

Sheila yanked her arm free. "Save it," she snapped. "I haven't got so desperate that I need consoling from a guy who might be wearing handcuffs any minute!"

"Have it your way," Max replied peaceably, watching her face. "But I have a feeling you're not as tough as you pretend to be, Detective. Am I right?"

She didn't answer. But from the look she cast up at him, Max could see that he'd hit the nail right on the head—and it scared the hell out of her.

Two

On Saturday night, Sheila showed up at the Tenth Precinct wearing her black leather miniskirt and a fuchsia sweater that showed off what little cleavage she could boast of.

Cowboy whistled when he saw her come up the steps of the precinct house. He was lounging against the door smoking a cigar and said, "Hubba, hubba."

"You silver-tongued devil, I bet your wife can hardly wait for you to get home at night."

"You're right about that!" Cowboy waggled his eyebrows and held the door open for Sheila. They went inside, walked past the muster desk where Sergeant Donohoe was reading a fishing magazine.

As they started up the steps together, Cowboy said, "So how come you're dressed like Jezebel tonight, Malone? Not that I'm complaining."

"I was working, of course."

"Where?"

"Guys across town needed a decoy at a supermarket."
She shrugged. "Some kids are beating up women in the
parking lot for their grocery money, so I hung around
waiting to get punched by a punk. No luck. I think we
scared them off. One cop practically wore his badge."

Cowboy was frowning. "I thought you were going to
take some time off from that stuff."

"Why would I?"

Her partner stopped on the landing and turned on Sheila,
blocking her way. He was a tall, wiry guy with a hound-dog
face and perceptive brown eyes. His voice could also drop
to a soft murmur when he wanted it to. He said, "You
don't have to play tough with me, Sheila. You need a break
after what happened."

"It happens to every cop," she answered shortly. "It was
my turn, that's all. I'll get over it."

He put his hand out to stop her from brushing past him
and got a solid grip on her forearm. "You were shook up
last night— I know you were. Holding an empty gun on
that Bollinger guy wasn't exactly the act of a sane woman."

"I'm perfectly sane. I just— We weren't supposed to be
on duty last night, so I didn't bother to load the damn
thing—"

"Is it loaded now?"

"What *is* this? The third degree?"

"It was a simple question. Is your gun loaded now?"

"Cowboy—"

"Look, you lucked out with Bollinger last night. He
could just as easily have turned out to be some drugged-up
kid with an Uzi instead of Cary Grant. Are you carrying a
useful weapon or not, partner? *My* life might depend on
it."

Sheila sighed. "All right. I'll load it."

Cowboy blew a sigh and raked his fingers through his thinning hair. "Look, it's going to be rough, I know. I know because I've been there. You can pretend for a while that nothing's different, but it's going to catch up with you, babe. You shot the guy. He deserved it. It was either you or him, and you won."

It was hard to explain, but Sheila didn't want to talk about her experience with other male cops. The men just didn't react the way she had to pulling the trigger. She wasn't quite sure exactly what her reaction was yet, but she did know that she didn't want to listen to any more I've-been-there stories.

She put her hand on her partner's sleeve, unable to look him in the eye. "I appreciate your concern, really I do, but I— I just can't think in gunfighter logic, Greg. No offense."

"Hey, that's cool, but—"

"I'll handle it my own way, all right? Just let me do my job for now. I promise I won't put you in jeopardy."

He nodded. "Okay. But I'm here, you know, when you're ready to talk."

Sheila smiled at her partner—a man who'd stayed with her for hours the night of the shooting. She had known it was his wife's birthday, but Cowboy hadn't gone home until the next morning. He'd slept on the sofa in Sheila's apartment, saying he wanted to keep an eye on her for a while.

"I know you're here for me," she said. "I just— I'm not ready yet, that's all."

He shrugged and released her arm with a pat. "Okay. Let me know when you want to yell and scream. I can take it. I'm married to Jenny, right?"

He put his arm across her shoulders and they went up the steps and into the squad room together.

The squad room was about fifteen feet wide and twice that long, packed with too many desks, too few chairs that the detectives fought over, a bunch of telephones that always seemed to be ringing, and not much fresh air.

Lieutenant Fiske was on the phone. The rest of the night shift was gathered around one of the desks. Jerry Piccolo and Marty Grimes were eating pizza from a box and kidding each other about women, their usual topic of conversation. Piccolo and Grimes acted like morons around the precinct house, but they were at the top of Sheila's list of cops to call when the chips were down.

Piccolo was saying, "Your date had a mustache like my old man, Grimes!"

"Who was that hunk of woman I saw *you* with last weekend, Pic? A lady wrestler or something? Oh, hell, Cowboy, put that cigar out before I call the fire department! What a stink!"

"Hey, Malone. Wow! Nice legs. Where'd you get stockings like that?"

"Why, you want to try on a pair, Piccolo?"

The lieutenant slammed down the telephone. "This is all I need!" He got up and started pacing, still scribbling in his notebook. "Of all nights, I'm stuck with you guys—two jerks who can't keep their pants zipped, a horse cop who's lonesome for an *animal*, for God's sake, and the only good Irish cop in the bunch is a damned *girl*!"

"Woman," corrected Cowboy.

"Girl," Sheila amended. "I don't mind being called a girl."

"Yeah, how old are you, Malone?" Grimes asked. "Pushing thirty yet?"

"You oughtta quit this job and start keeping a hubby warm at night."

"Shut up," snapped Cowboy.

The lieutenant's face was purple. "We've got work to do here!"

"What's the word, oh fearless one?" Cowboy asked, draping himself across an empty desk like a pinup posing for a centerfold.

"Too much," replied the lieutenant. "That call just now was an armed robbery. Two juveniles toting water pistols just held up a laundromat, except the victim didn't *know* they were water pistols until he almost had a heart attack. Cripes Almighty, what's this neighborhood coming to? Kids playing for real! Grimes and Piccolo, you take it." He ripped a page from his notebook and tossed it at them.

While they gathered up their jackets to leave, snatching the last two pieces of pizza to eat in the car, Fiske turned to Cowboy and Sheila. "In the meantime, you two talk to me about last night."

"What about it?"

Lieutenant Fiske perched his bulk on the edge of one of the desks. "The Bollinger break-in."

"It's actually the Pletheridge break-in," Sheila corrected. "Max doesn't live in the house, he was just passing through." She realized her partner was looking at her strangely at the use of Max Bollinger's first name, so she added quickly, "He might have stolen the jewelry himself and faked the break-in."

"What makes you say that?"

"His hand was cut up, like maybe he'd smashed the kitchen window with it. Also, he's been in some kind of trouble before. He wouldn't say too much about that, and since we were just doing preliminary—"

"Yeah, yeah, so what's your gut feeling? Did the guy steal his mother's goodies?"

Sheila hesitated, and Cowboy laughed. "Don't ask her. The guy looks like a movie star—complete with hot temper and smoldering looks. Her tongue was hanging out."

"It was not!"

"All right, it wasn't, but it should have been if you were in your right mind. The guy's a charmer, Lieutenant. Smooth and cool. I wouldn't be surprised if he did pull the job himself and then hung around the house to be discovered taking a hot shower afterward."

Fiske turned a sharp eye on Sheila. "Malone? What do you think?"

She shrugged. "Cowboy's right. He's a smooth customer. And smart."

"Maybe not too smart," said Fiske. "Some cop from the Third Precinct called. They want your help again tonight."

"Oh, yeah?" Cowboy propped himself on one elbow. "What for?"

"The jewelry Mrs. Pletheridge reported stolen? It turned up in a hockshop downtown today."

"That was quick," Sheila said.

"Too quick," agreed the lieutenant. "A sure sign that amateurs are involved. They want you, Malone, to help them pick up Bollinger for questioning tonight."

Sheila felt herself start to blush for no good reason. "Why me?"

"The usual. They want a woman decoy planted in an alley—"

"Hold it," Cowboy interrupted. "What happened to giving her a break from that detail for a while?"

The lieutenant sighed. "When a cop looks like Malone, she's going to get used for this kind of work, Stankowsky. She knew it coming into this job, and you've been around long enough to understand the facts of life, too. If she's got a complaint—"

"I'll make it myself," Sheila said quickly. "It's okay with me, Lieutenant. I don't mind. But why do the Third Precinct guys need a hooker on this job? If they're just picking him up for questioning—"

"He's at the opera." Lieutenant Fiske rolled his eyes. "And the TV people just broke the story about the jewelry on the seven o'clock news. A bunch of reporters have roared over to the opera house to grab Bollinger for quotes at halftime. The cops at the Third think he's going to duck out once he hears the news."

"So? They grab him in the lobby. How tough can that be?"

The lieutenant smiled coldly. "You know who Bollinger is? And the Pletheridge dame? I'll tell you. They used to give money by the truckload to political campaigns. *Two* guys on the city council have asked that Bollinger and his mum get treated with kid gloves. So, no arrests made in front of TV cameras."

"So we pick them up the honest way? Snatch him sneaking out the stage door?"

Fiske lifted his massive shoulders. "I'm not giving the orders on this one, Malone. You want the job?"

"What about me?" Cowboy asked. "Am I going, too?"

"I need you here, Stankowsky. What am I supposed to do if there's a real crime committed in my own precinct?"

"I want to be with my partner."

"She's a big girl, Cowboy. Let her do her job."

Sheila left before she got any more static from her partner.

There were no cars available at the precinct garage because of budget cuts and an accident yesterday in which a plainclothes cop ran smack into a utility pole. He admitted he'd been watching two college girls jogging at the time. Sheila took her own car and drove over to the opera house. She couldn't find a parking space within a mile of the place, so she left the little car around the corner with two wheels up on the sidewalk and walked to the front of the ornate building.

She recognized the cop in charge of the operation. His name was Larson, and in spite of his weasel face and mean way of talking to subordinates, he was a decent man. He didn't leer down her sweater or waste time making remarks about her legs; instead, he told Sheila to keep an eye on the alley behind the opera house.

"He might go out the back once he sees the crowd of reporters in the lobby. If he does, stop him. You know what Bollinger looks like?"

"Yes," Sheila replied. She almost added, "All over."

The alley was well lighted, but littered with garbage from an overflowing dumpster. The trash was mostly paper, however, and didn't smell. But a Chinese restaurant also backed onto the alley, and the fragrances that wafted from the kitchen reminded Sheila that she hadn't had time for dinner.

She strolled up and down the mouth of the alley to stay warm and to keep one eye on the activity along the side of the opera house. After twenty minutes, a group of elegantly dressed men and women came out an exit door and stood on the sidewalk, lighting up cigarettes and talking together. Sheila assumed that intermission had started.

In another minute, a short man wearing a watch cap hurried up the sidewalk toward her, and Sheila recognized him at once. He was a reporter, a man from the city newspaper who sometimes covered the courtroom news. She'd seen him when she'd testified a few times at the county courthouse and knew he had a reputation for supporting stiff sentences for all kinds of crime, regardless of circumstances.

"Hey, baby," she hailed him, praying he wasn't going to recognize her in the decoy getup she was wearing. "You looking for some action, sweetheart?"

Seeing Sheila in the alley, the reporter stopped dead on the sidewalk. He looked outraged for a moment, but as Sheila approached, he began to lose his nerve. He answered, "Yeah, I'm looking for a guy."

"Not my department, sweetie," Sheila called back, smiling broadly and rolling her hips as she strolled closer to the man. With luck, she could drive him out of the alley with obnoxiousness. "You sure I can't make you happy?"

"No. I— I thought maybe he'd come out back here. We've lost him, you see."

"Baby, there's nobody here but me. Can't we negotiate a little? I can play any part you want—"

"No, no." The little reporter backed up on the sidewalk. "That's okay. I just thought— Well, I'll go look for him someplace else."

"I'll be here if you can't find him, sugar."

The reporter fled—and just in time. Sheila turned at the sound of a door creaking open, and through the darkness, she spotted two figures exiting the opera house into the alley. A man and a woman shut the door behind them and quickly strode up the alley toward Sheila. The man had his hand snugly around the woman's elbow, and he was hustling her along and buttoning his coat with his other hand at the same time. Sheila caught a glimpse of a tuxedo under his coat. The woman was wearing a black velvet dress held up by nothing but her breasts. She had a fur cape flung around her shoulders and wore a pair of shoes that could have qualified as instruments of torture in another culture. Her shocking blond hair was cut short to show off a set of enormous diamond earrings. At least, Sheila assumed they were diamonds. The blonde didn't look like the rhinestone type.

When the man realized they weren't alone in the alley and lifted his head, Sheila saw that it was Max Bollinger.

"Hey, Slick," she greeted as the couple drew closer. "Didn't you like the show?"

Max Bollinger halted in the middle of the alley, dragging his companion to a ragged stop beside him. They both looked elegantly surprised—the cat burglar and his moll. Max stared at Sheila, his gaze flicking down her outfit and lingering for just a split second on her legs before returning to her face. His eyes narrowed in disbelief. "Detective Malone? Is that you?"

"We meet again," Sheila said, strolling closer. In a tuxedo, Max looked even sexier than he had in the shower. Sheila felt a quiver of response inside herself and tried to subdue it quickly. "This time you're a little warmer, I assume."

"You're not," he remarked. "Don't the police have regulations concerning skirt lengths?"

"Darling," said the woman by Max's side. Her voice was low and lilting with the hint of a German accent. "Will you introduce me to your friend?"

"She's a police officer, Elke."

"That's right," Sheila replied, showing her badge and feeling absurdly infuriated that she looked like a harridan in front of Max's beautiful date. "I'm very sorry to cut your evening short like this, Elke, but Mr. Bollinger's presence is requested elsewhere."

"Where?" Max asked at once.

"You want me to spell it out?"

Impatient, he demanded, "Am I being arrested?"

"Nothing like that. It's just a quiet question-and-answer session, that's all."

"Now? This minute?"

"Yep."

"Let me take Elke back to her hotel first, will you?"

Sheila glanced at the other woman's curious expression and shook her head. "I can't risk it. You might decide to skip town, and I'd—"

"I won't do anything of the kind. Give me half an hour."

"Sorry, Slick. Either you come with me now or I turn you over to the guys out front."

"What guys?"

"The cops and the press. They're waiting for you—but I suppose you figured that. Why else would you be ducking out the back door?"

Max glowered, then said shortly, "I'll go with you." He dug into the pockets of his black cashmere coat and came up with a set of car keys. He took Elke's hand and dropped the keys into her palm. "I'm sorry about this," he said to her. "I'll fill you in later, if you don't mind. Can you drive yourself back to your hotel? Or should I get you a cab?"

Elke smiled graciously at him and closed her long fingers around the keys. "You know I can't pass up a chance to drive your car, Max."

He tried to smile back at her. "I figured it was the only reason you came out with me tonight."

"Call me as soon as you can."

Sheila said, "Don't wait up, Elke."

"I'll call," Max promised.

Elke gave Sheila a narrow look before spinning on her heel and stalking out of the alley. Sheila felt ashamed of herself. She'd been petulant just because Elke's cosmopolitan manner had rubbed her the wrong way.

But she quickly gathered her composure. Sheila turned to Max and said, "She's very good-looking, Slick. Is she a steady girlfriend?"

"A business associate," Max corrected, thrusting his hands into the pockets of his coat and looking none too pleased to see Elke leaving. "I like doing business with her more than anyone else I know."

"I can see why," Sheila retorted before she could stop herself. "Shall we walk to my car?"

"No handcuffs?" Max asked as they fell into step together. "Aren't you supposed to read me my rights?"

"That comes later. You're being invited to the station house to answer a few questions."

He cast a glance at her. "Can you give me a clue what this is all about?"

"Sorry, I'm just here to deliver you to the precinct."

"Am I going to be worked over with a rubber hose?"

"I don't know. Rubber hoses aren't my specialty."

"What's your best guess, then? Tell me what's going on."

"Neither one of us should be doing any talking without your attorney present, Slick."

"That's a very annoying name, you know. I thought we introduced ourselves last night. Surely you can call me Max without violating police procedure."

Sheila's car was still where she'd left it, and nobody had come along and ticketed it. She unlocked the passenger door and opened it. "Okay, Max, hop in."

He stood on the sidewalk looking at her battered little car as though it were a device left over from the Spanish Inquistion. "No human being could 'hop' into that car without breaking both legs in the process. Is this a police vehicle?"

"It's mine, as a matter of fact."

"How can a woman as tall as you are fit into this machine?"

"Just get in, will you? It's a short ride."

"Maybe you could just handcuff me to the roof?"

"Everybody's a comedian. Get in."

Sheila slid in behind the wheel and shoved the key into the ignition. Eventually, Max wedged his tall frame into the passenger seat.

He slammed the door with a muffled sound of pain and turned his shoulder to the window. "At least I get to watch you drive in that outfit." He peered at her short skirt and loose sweater. "What are you wearing, anyway? That isn't how you were dressed last night."

"It's a disguise, of course. Fasten your seat belt."

He reached for the belt and began wrestling with it. "Let me guess—"

"I was a decoy tonight. That's all you need to know."

"Who was the lucky target?"

"Nobody from your social circle, I'm sure. Usually the criminal element comes from the other side of the golf course."

He was still struggling with the seat belt. "Usually?"

She reached across and pulled the seat belt tight, then buckled it with a snap. "We don't see you upper-crust types unless it's court day. Why is it that all judges wear cashmere coats like yours?"

"Maybe they get a group discount. You're awfully touchy tonight, Detective."

"Let's call it maintaining a professional distance."

"Either that or you don't like me very much. Is that possible?"

"You sound surprised. Do you consider yourself irresistible?"

"Most women give me half a chance before they start getting hostile. You, on the other hand, seem determined to keep me at arm's length."

"Don't worry. A set of handcuffs has a way of getting two people very close indeed."

"You think I'm going to be handcuffed before this night is over?"

"You tell me."

When he didn't answer, Sheila started the car with a roar. It was long past the time when she should have replaced her muffler, but Max Bollinger had the grace to pretend to ignore the sound. Either that, or he was genuinely starting to worry about getting arrested. When she pulled into the street and glanced at him to figure it out, he was smiling at her.

"You're a unique woman, Detective Malone."

"Don't try to snow me, Max."

"I'm being serious. I don't think I've ever met a woman like you. So strong and so beautiful at the same time."

"You have a thing for miniskirts and fishnet stockings?"

"I'm not looking at the clothes at the moment. You have an angelic face, did you know that?"

She gave a little laugh. "Want to see my tattoo?"

"I'd be surprised if you really had one—unless it's a subtle little rose painted on your shoulder. And I'll bet it's an attractive shoulder indeed."

Sheila drove down the street and around the corner. "Listen, Max, you might as well lay off the sweet talk. I can't help you tonight, okay?"

"Stop being so suspicious. I think you're an attractive woman—it's as simple as that. And if you hadn't dashed off so quickly last night, we could have gotten to know each other better. It was just getting interesting when—"

"I should have kept my mouth shut last night."

"But you didn't, and I'm glad. I just wish we hadn't gotten off on the wrong foot."

"We're not off on any foot!"

"I think we could enjoy each other's company," Max pressed. "Why don't we have dinner after I'm finished answering questions?"

"You don't give up, do you?"

"Never say die," he said with a low laugh.

Sheila steeled herself against his charm. A good cop never let herself be manipulated by a charming suspect.

Well . . . almost never, she thought. If she'd been honest, she would have admitted that her instincts had seemed fogged ever since she'd laid eyes on Max Bollinger. There was something about the man that she didn't trust, but she wasn't sure it had anything to do with criminal tendencies. Besides, how could any woman not be distracted by Max's sexy demeanor?

With a swerve, she pulled her car into the No Parking zone in front of the opera house. A few people were milling around there, and Sheila spotted a television van right away. At the sight of it, Max stiffened beside her. She heard him mutter quietly.

Without turning off the engine, Sheila rolled down the car window to address the uniformed cop standing there. She showed him her badge and said, "Tell Larson I have his man. He can catch up with us at the precinct."

The cop took a look into the car at Max, then straightened and solemnly waved Sheila past. She pulled out into the street and headed north.

"Thanks," said Max, relaxing again. "I don't know why the news media finds me so fascinating."

"A rich man rips off his mother's jewelry, maybe?"

His voice hardened. "Do you think I stole her jewelry?"

"I've met some very nice people who turned out to be pretty rotten criminals."

Max wondered what kind of people the lovely Detective Malone met in her line of work. She didn't always seem like the hard case she pretended to be. How did she cope?

As they roared along in her noisy, uncomfortable car, he found himself wondering a lot of things about her, in fact.

But first he had his own neck to worry about, so he said, "You must have developed some instincts over the years. What do you think? Am I guilty or not?"

She glanced at him—green eyes amused and knowledgeable at the same time. She said, "Let's just drop it. I'm not in the mood to wrangle with you."

Max shrugged. "Okay. But tell me—is your mood a result of what happened to you earlier this week? The shooting?"

"My mood is none of your business."

"It bothers the hell out of you, doesn't it?"

She didn't speak. She concentrated on driving the little car across a bridge to the downtown section of the city.

"The shooting, I mean," Max went on cautiously. "How did it happen?"

"I don't want to rehash anything with you, pal. No offense, but you couldn't possibly comprehend my work."

"Try me."

She shook her head. "I hang around dark streets posing as a decoy for every kind of crazy that preys on women around the city. I meet a kind of citizen you probably never dreamed exists—folks who wouldn't be caught dead hanging out at the opera house, believe me."

"I don't, either—not all the time. Where did it happen?"

She sighed testily. "Up near the university."

"You were some kind of decoy?"

"Yeah. We were trying to catch a punk who raped three students at gunpoint. One in August, one in January, and another girl in February. He tried again a week ago, only the girl fought him off.

"Brave girl."

"Amen. She was blind, actually, and didn't realize he had a gun."

"He attacked a blind girl?" Max asked, appalled.

"He wasn't particularly choosy. He had a system—picking off girls who were walking back to the dormitories from night classes. The fact that he carried a gun made the decoy idea a little hairy, but we figured it was our best alternative. Another cop and I took turns walking through the park every night for two weeks."

Max watched her face as she drove, marveling at the way she could recite the facts—facts that were the stuff of nightmares for most women. "Weren't you scared?"

She shrugged. "Sure. But fear keeps you alert. Anyway, he jumped me on Tuesday. We struggled a little—"

"Struggled?"

"He hit me a couple of times." Sheila brushed her hand into the ponytail that cascaded down the side of her face onto her shoulder. She held up the ponytail so that Max could get a look at the side of her jaw and her ear—the places where the rapist had apparently clubbed her with his gun. The bruises were bright green, and the sight of them suddenly made Max feel absurdly sick.

"See?" she asked.

Max cursed softly.

"No big deal," she said, dropping her hair and struggling to keep her voice cool. Max thought he heard her falter, however, as she added, "I got a few licks in myself, but it—things went bad. Another cop started yelling from across the park, and I could see—I knew by his eyes—that he was going to shoot me. I guess he figured it would be better to kill me so I couldn't tell anyone what he looked like. So I— I reacted.''

"You shot him instead.''

She nodded. Pulling the car through a set of wrought-iron gates, she applied the brakes. ''I didn't think I had a choice. I got the first shot off, but he pulled his trigger, too. The bullet went right past my throat and into the ground beside me.'' She laughed uncertainly. ''My ear is still ringing from that one!''

Max stared at her, realizing that she'd been right—he didn't have any idea what her work was like. He forced himself to ask, ''He's dead?''

''Oh, you bet. He fell on top of me, bled all over my clothes and hair.'' Gripping the steering wheel tightly and looking visibly shaken, she went on. ''Boy, you don't know how many times I've wished I could live that ten seconds over again!''

''What would you do differently?''

''I don't know.'' Her hold on the steering wheel made her knuckles blanch. ''Something.''

A moment later she'd pulled herself together and was looking around the precinct parking lot for a space to put the car. There was a slot at the end of the line marked Lieutenant Sardino. She pulled into it, set the hand brake and shut off the engine.

Max said, ''If we all had second chances, the world would be a better place.''

''Making the world a better place is supposed to be my job.''

"Well, you've certainly made some progress toward that goal. You saved some poor college kid from getting herself—"

"I know, I know. But I wish I didn't feel so rotten about it!"

After a silence, Max reached across and tweaked Sheila's hair back over the bruise on her neck. "I'd be scared if you could brush it off easily."

Did a shine of tears suddenly appear in her lovely green eyes? Max couldn't be sure. In the next instant, she shoved her door open and got out of the car. Max followed her tall, stiffly erect figure into the brick building that housed the Third Precinct. Some other cops immediately recognized and hailed her in a friendly way. Sheila reacted with a couple of off-color suggestions that drew laughter as she headed farther down a hallway. Eventually she found the police officers who were ready to question Max.

Seeing the phalanx of stern-faced detectives, Max felt a queasy sensation start to build in his stomach, but he put the interview out of his head for a second and caught Sheila's arm before she left him alone.

"Stick around," he said to her under his breath. "This won't take long."

"Then what?" she asked, trying to look amused again.

"I'll take you out for dinner when I'm finished."

"Only if they don't arrest you first."

He grinned at her. "They won't."

Three

The lieutenant in command of the Third was fixing himself a cup of coffee, so Sheila strolled over and tried to pump him for news on the Pletheridge break-in.

He pulled rank and gave her a lofty look. "Information on that case is on a need-to-know basis, I'm afraid."

Sheila ordered herself not to remind the stuffed shirt that the case had started out as hers. He was the type to accuse her of insubordination, so she steamed in silence. Then he had the gall to take a slug of coffee and ask Sheila to stick around while Max was being questioned.

"He lives in your precinct," the lieutenant explained, not in the least embarrassed about asking Sheila for a favor. "You could take him home. You'll save one of my men a trip."

His tone of voice indicated that the time of any of his hardworking men was far more important than hers. Sheila ground her teeth. She could have refused, of course. She could have claimed she was needed back at her own station house. But she didn't. And she told herself it was only because the lieutenant had asked so nicely, when in fact her reason was far more personal.

She was hanging around drinking a cup of terrible coffee, when Sally Marshall turned up. A public defender, Sally had graduated from the law school where Sheila was taking classes. They stood around shooting the breeze for a few minutes.

"How's the job?" Sheila asked, eager to hear how Sally was making use of her new degree.

"The job is great. But," she added bitterly, "it's the rest of my life that's a mess. My husband can't stand my new hours. I spend all my time in this dump talking to dope peddlers, and Oliver thinks I ought to be at home making gourmet dinners and sipping wine by the fire, listening to him talk about *his* job."

"Any change takes some getting used to."

"Yeah, but you have to be willing to change, and he's not." Sally gulped coffee as if it were a much-needed martini. "I don't care. I'm going to make this job work for me."

Sheila heard the determination in Sally's voice, but her body language told another story. "I'm sure Oliver will realize how important it is to you."

"Let's hope he figures it out soon," Sally muttered. Then she pulled herself together. "Anyway, my job is really challenging, Sheila. I'm the new kid on the block, so I get stuck with the really lousy cases, but I'm learning *and* building a reputation as a lady who's not afraid of anything. The D.A. has his eye on me, I think."

"Sounds promising."

"It is. He's looking for more women in his office. I'm glad I quit my teaching job to finish my degree. Let me give you some advice, okay? Finish your courses as quickly as you can. Taking a couple of classes every semester is the hard way to get on the fast track. Besides,'' Sally added, ''you'll live longer if you get out of your line of work.''

Sheila ruminated about that advice while she finished her coffee.

Eventually, the interrogation room opened and a flood of detectives came out. Among them was Max Bollinger. He didn't look the least bit ruffled by his questioning. In fact, from the way everybody was behaving, it looked like he'd given a party instead of endured a tough grilling by the cops. All the men were laughing and joshing like a bunch of cronies leaving their club after a good card game. Max had managed to charm the lot of them. The sight of him started Sheila's heart doing flip-flops, too.

He spotted Sheila lingering by the coffee machine and spoke loudly enough for all the cops to hear: ''Ah, here's my date. I'd better not keep her waiting any longer, right?''

Sheila felt her face turn pink with mortification as the cops burst into hearty ho-ho-ho's and a few bawdy jokes at her expense. But she determined not to let Max Bollinger see her discomfiture.

''Well,'' he said lightly, slipping on his coat as he strode up to her, ''they tell me I'm free to go as long as I don't make any trips to South America.''

''That's better than getting arrested on the spot, I guess.''

He stopped to button his coat and gave her his best movie-star smile. ''You're still here, I notice. Because of me?''

Just as archly, she replied, ''I thought you might need someone to hold your hand after the inquisition.''

''It wasn't too unpleasant. But I'd like holding hands with you, anyway, Detective.''

"Don't hold your breath. Actually, I've been ordered to take you home. They must be worried about the South American jaunt."

"It's your duty to see me home, eh? Well, what about dinner first?" He took her arm and guided Sheila down the steps of the precinct house. "We could try the seafood place around the corner. It's still there, isn't it?"

"It is, but I'm on a diet."

He cast a grin at the long expanse of her legs. "You shouldn't be."

Sheila disengaged her arm on the pretext of digging her car keys from her pocket. "Let's just proceed directly to your doorstep, all right? I have no intention of having dinner with you, Max. Where are we going exactly? The lieutenant tells me you aren't living with your mother anymore."

"Would you live with Angela Pletheridge if you didn't have to?"

"From the way I found you last night, I had the impression you were moving in."

"I just stopped by to say hello and pick up the keys to my new place. I used the shower because I wasn't sure what kind of condition I'd find the apartment in."

"Your apartment doesn't have running water? Isn't that kind of a nuisance?"

He laughed easily. "It does have water and all the other services, but I wasn't positive. It's a unique place I'm renovating. You'll like it, I think. It's a little unusual on the inside at the moment, but—"

"Who says I'm going to see the inside?"

Max grinned. "You will."

Sheila drove, and they bantered awhile. Sheila had to admit that she enjoyed talking with Max. He was quick and amusing, and she found herself forgetting her troubles. It took all her concentration to fend off his flirtations.

Under her command, the little car shot across one of the city's many old bridges and roared into the South Side, a neighborhood in the old style—lots of narrow streets that ran along the river, and a population that was a mixture of many ethnic groups. For generations, a comfortable melting-pot spirit had bonded South Side community together.

Passing a bus stop crowded with men carrying lunch boxes home from work even at that late hour, Sheila couldn't help asking, "This neighborhood isn't exactly your style, is it?"

"What do you mean?"

"It's— Well, we don't have a country club in the South Side. Why are you living over here and not in some shiny Yuppie condo across town?"

"It's where I work," Max answered simply.

"You work?" Sheila retorted.

He laughed. "Do you imagine that I'm some kind of idle rich playboy? Dilettante of the Western world? Of course I work! The brewery is over there."

Sheila threaded her car around a pizza delivery truck parked outside one of the row houses on Carson Street. "The old brewery, you mean? It's been closed for years."

"We're opening again."

"No kidding?" The closing of Bollinger's Brewery, the original makers of Steel City Ale, had been one of the great tragedies Sheila remembered from her younger days. How many of her father's friends had been put out of work when the old brewery closed? How many families had been plunged into terrible financial straits? She could vividly remember the pall of desperation that had settled over the South Side when hundreds of men were laid off from their jobs.

Max relaxed as best he could in the small seat and began to talk about his plans for reopening his family's company. "Several years ago, my father was forced to sell the Bollinger name to a German beer manufacturer. It was the only asset left after we went bankrupt. Part of the deal, however, included my going to work for the Germans—it was something my father felt he had to give me when the rest of my inheritance was used to bail out the company the last time. For a few years I was the Germans' representative in this country, then I went to Hamburg to study the business from that end. I convinced them to let me try once more over here, so I'm making arrangements to start up the brewery again."

Musingly, Sheila said, "That will make a big difference in the economy around here."

"Yes, there's an excellent labor force available in this city."

She heard the casual note in his voice and said sharply, "I hope you plan to make things last this time. I don't think the people of the neighborhood could stand another depression like the one we had when the brewery closed. You'd better stay in business for a long time if you expect people to depend on you for their livelihood."

Max turned his head to watch her face as she drove. "Believe me, I wouldn't be risking so much myself if I was only looking at the short term. Here, take a left up at this corner."

Sheila obeyed, pulling her car into an alley that was roughly paved with bricks. The towering walls of the old Bollinger's Brewery rose to the right, casting dark shadows into the alley.

"Stop a minute," Max said, and Sheila applied the brakes.

"Let's get out here," he said. "Do you mind?"

He was already out of the car before Sheila could reply, so she finished pulling the car to one side of the dark alley and shut off the engine. When she got out, Max was standing in the middle of the narrow street with his hands shoved into the deep pockets of his coat to ward off the cold as he stared up at the high brick walls that rose around them. Someone had used a can of spray paint to scrawl graffiti on the bricks, but Max didn't appear to see that.

His breath clouded the chill March air as he said, "This building was constructed by my grandfather. He chose this site because it's so close to the river, see? That was when he used to ship hops by boat. *His* father was an old, old man at that time—practically an invalid—who'd come to this country with his son, but the old coot was a bricklayer by trade, and he helped lay the brick of these walls, even though he was nearly eighty years old."

Standing in that freezing alley, Sheila watched Max's face as he spoke. His smile was different as he talked about his family. It was more genuine, perhaps—as though those memories sprang from a special part of his heart.

Mindless of the few flakes of snow that filtered down from the dark sky, he continued, "The brewery was passed on to my father in the fifties, and he added that addition a few years later."

Sheila peered in the direction Max pointed. "The larger building?"

"Yes, the stone one nearer the railroad tracks. That project was my father's pride and joy. But the industry started to change soon after it was built, and my father couldn't keep the business profitable. It was his fault that he didn't stay on top of things—and the economic climate of the time was against him, too. After nearly a decade of fighting, he lost the fortune his father had passed to him."

"Where were you when that happened?"

"In college. I never finished—we ran out of tuition money, and I was needed to help keep things afloat a little longer." He spoke without a trace of bitterness. "But we lost everything, and my father..."

Sheila heard his voice trail off. She prompted, "Your father?"

"He died a few months after we settled the bankruptcy. Now I'm back at square one."

Starting to understand the gleam of pride she'd seen in Max's expression, Sheila said, "With the buildings your grandfather put here."

Max pulled himself back on track. "Yes, but now they're owned by a big German conglomerate and I've got to work like hell to get everything back into the family."

"That's your plan?"

"You'd better believe it. Maybe it's a foolish dream, but I can't help it. To give up and let these buildings crumble seems—well—damned weak."

"You're not going to let it happen, are you?"

He said firmly, "Nothing's going to stop me." A gleam burned in Max's eyes as he gazed at the bricks laid by his great-grandfather.

For a moment Sheila wondered how far Max Bollinger would go to achieve his dream. Would he stoop to stealing his mother's jewelry to finance the opening of the family business?

He turned to look at her and flashed a charming smile again. "What are you thinking?"

Startled out of her thoughts, Sheila said, "What?"

"You have a decidedly curious expression on your face, Detective Malone."

She allowed a grin. "I'm trained to look curious all the time—Sherlock Holmes, you know. Don't let it bother you. Shall we go?"

"Out for dinner?"

"No," she answered patiently. "To your doorstep. I'd like to get back to my precinct house before midnight. Can you manage to get into my car again?"

"No need," he replied, striding across the alley, shoes crunching on the icy patches. "My place is right over here."

Too intrigued to stop herself, Sheila followed Max across the snow-dusted bricks to a wide doorway hidden in the shadows. It looked like a freight entrance with a single-panel door cut in the middle of it.

Max rattled a set of keys as he spoke. "I'm planning to have some decent lights installed, but these things take time. At the moment, the lack of security precautions just makes the place look empty. At least, that's what I'm hoping. Here we go."

He unlocked the heavy door, and it swung inward. "I'll lead the way, if you don't mind," he said, preceding her into the darkness.

Sheila stepped over the threshold and into a cavernous garage. By the moonlight that penetrated the frosty windows, she could make out the shapes of an old truck and what looked like a huge wagon.

Sheila stumbled against one of its big wheels. "What in the world is this?"

In the dark beside her, Max laughed. "Terrific, isn't it? It's a beer wagon. When I was a kid, we sent this rig to parades all over the state. We had a team of black horses and a Dalmatian dog that rode in the back, and I used to get to sit beside the driver and throw lollipops. Maybe someday I'll get it fixed and repainted. It's fifty years old, at least."

Sheila could make out the words on the side of the wagon: Bollinger's Premium Steel City Ale. The paint was faded and flaking in places, but the curly letters were still full of pride.

"This way," Max called.

She followed him up a short flight of steps to another door, which he unlocked and pushed wide. Reaching inside, he found a switch, and a flood of bright light nearly blinded Sheila.

"Watch your step," Max cautioned. "The workmen leave junk all over the place."

Max's apartment was the upstairs loft above the garage—a huge expanse of space that echoed with their footsteps. A dozen enormous windows ran along the north wall, no doubt providing a wash of sunlight all day long, but at the moment reflecting the light from a series of brass sconces mounted on the pillars that bisected the space in a dramatic straight line. The wooden floor had been polished and varnished recently, and the brick walls had been sandblasted until they looked spanking new. The place was larger than a high-school gymnasium.

"What do you think?" Max asked.

"Wow!" was all Sheila could manage at first. "It looks like a movie set."

The workmen had left a clutter of tools and materials at one end of the long room, but otherwise the place was as eerie as an empty stadium. The kitchen was still rough, but dominated by a brick hearth and a large brass pot-rack, now empty.

Letting her gaze travel around the huge loft, Sheila spotted a cluster of furniture jammed into one distant corner. By instinct, she headed in that direction.

Max strolled after her. "Most of the furniture came from my father's place. It's been in storage for years, but I had it all delivered here this morning. I need to go through it to decide what I can throw away."

Sheila glanced at the heap of papers and notebooks piled on one of the tables. "Looks like you've got your work cut out for you."

With a smooth wave, Max swept the papers into one huge stack. Sheila wondered fleetingly if he was trying to hide something from her. His voice sounded normal when he said "This project is going to take a while, all right. I wanted to finish it in a couple of days, but I've been busy doing other things."

"Like going to the opera?"

He laughed, turning her away from the papers and shrugging off his coat. He draped it over a chair. "That was business, you know. Elke works for the Germans, too."

Sheila glanced back at the heap of furniture piled in the corner. Though all the pieces were old, she could see that they had been expensive. The whole place looked expensive, in fact. Max Bollinger might be bankrupt, but he certainly didn't live in the style of a poverty-stricken person.

One impression seemed very obvious to Sheila. Not only was there very little heat in Max's apartment, but the empty expanse of the huge room felt as barren as windswept tundra—the perfect place for a lone wolf to roam.

Keeping her observations to herself, Sheila stuffed her cold hands into her pockets and remarked, "You're going to need a heck of a lot more stuff than this to fill up the place."

"Oh, I don't know. I kind of like the open feeling. You never know when you might feel like playing basketball in the middle of the night. I thought I'd put a hoop on that wall over there."

Amused at the thought of tuxedo-clad Max shooting hoops, Sheila asked, "Where will the swimming pool go?"

He sauntered closer, loosening his tie. "No pool, but I thought a Jacuzzi would be nice—when I can afford it."

"I'll come back," Sheila said lightly, "when it's installed."

Max stopped in front of her, gazing into her eyes with bold intimacy. "I hope you'll come back before that."

"To arrest you, maybe."

He smiled with charm and pointedly didn't deny the possibility. "We're not just going to have a professional relationship, are we, Sheila? Cop and suspect?"

"That's all I have in mind," she replied, standing her ground even as Max took one of her hands in his and began to caress the backs of her fingers with his thumb. His touch was gentle and seductive.

"My mind is full of a great many ideas where you're concerned," he said softly.

Sheila tried to pull her hand free. "Look, Max—"

"Why don't I call for some Chinese food?" he murmured before she could finish spelling out the reasons why any kind of relationship between them was absurd. "We could grab a few pillows, have a picnic on the floor and then...let nature take its course."

At least his proposition was straightforward, Sheila thought. A sleazier guy would have tried to manipulate her, but Max was direct and made no apologies for his methods. She liked him for that—and maybe for a few other things, too, if the truth were known.

But she responded coolly, "I think that's a little premature."

The flicker of pleasure in his eye grew. "But not impossible?"

She tried to pull away. "Impossible until the investigation is cleared up."

"Maybe I can give you some incentive to finish the investigation sooner than you might ordinarily."

Sheila cast a slanting look up at him. "What kind of incentive?"

"This," he answered, and bent closer.

His lips took hers in a quick but surprisingly gentle kiss that warmed Sheila's mouth and sent a rush of delicious sensations downward through her body. She blinked unsteadily when it was over and found herself staring into Max's amused and decidedly malevolent eyes. Gentleness was not what she'd expected from him, but Max was coaxing her, she realized—tantalizing her instead of roughly claiming what he wanted. With his fingertips he drew a slow circle on her cheek, watching her expression and promising something sweetly sensual with his enticing gaze.

Before she could muster a word of protest, he slipped his hands into her hair and tipped her face up to his, then swooped in for another kiss—longer this time, but no less gentle. His mouth was firm and potent, and Sheila found herself reacting by instinct alone. Her hands moved involuntarily to his chest, and beneath her palms only his crisp white shirt lay between her and his bare flesh.

Max parted her lips and found her tongue with his, rolling it sensually until Sheila felt dizzy. Common sense abandoned her for a moment, and she kissed him back. Her whole body grew so hot that Sheila wondered dimly why she'd ever thought his loft was cold. Her limbs were throbbing with the heat.

But at last Sheila fought down the boiling temperature inside herself and drew back. Maddeningly, she found she couldn't meet his gaze.

Max wondered if he'd ever known a woman so hard to figure out. One second she was cool and aloof, but in the blink of an eye she was kissing him until his toes curled. Now she was blushing—a lovely pink that colored her creamy skin. In the sizzling silence, Max wound one arm around her body, pulling Sheila closer against his frame. He nuzzled her earlobe with his mouth. "You don't know how much I've wanted to do that."

"Max," Sheila said, sounding nothing like a city police detective. "Stop."

"You don't really want me to."

"You feel good," she admitted unsteadily, "but I can't do this."

"You need it," he murmured against her throat. "You need lots of it, Sheila."

"No, I don't. Stop. I'm serious!"

"You're too serious. I can tell you're not usually as prim and proper as you've been pretending." He caressed her ribs with one hand, each stroke coming closer and closer to her breast. She shivered in his arms, but not from the cold. "You've had a rough week," he told her. "Well, so have I. We could make love right now and feel a hell of a lot better in the morning."

She couldn't help laughing. "You make it sound so logical."

"Come on, we could both use a night of misbehavior."

Carefully Sheila extricated herself from his embrace. "I don't think so, Max. We come from different worlds. It would never work."

Still relaxed, he allowed her to pull away. "Who's talking about a long-term love affair?"

She laughed shortly. "Well, that's one of our differences, then. Just because I'm dressed like a streetwalker doesn't mean I'm a one-night stand, Bollinger."

"Sheila—"

"Look," she snapped, her patience giving way, "maybe you're the son of a rich man, but that doesn't give you the right to assume I'll hit the sheets with you at the drop of a hat. I've been kissed by better men than you."

"I doubt it," Max retorted, not taking the least bit of offense. He knew she didn't mean a word of it. She lied badly.

Sheila spun around and headed for the door. "Good night," she called over her shoulder. "See you in court."

"Or sooner," Max called back.

Pleased with his night's work, Max locked the door after she'd gone and strolled back to the heap of papers he'd hastily concealed from Sheila's seemingly casual study. He pulled one of the notebooks free from the pile and flipped it open randomly.

"Damn," he muttered, staring at the meaningless column of figures so carefully recorded by his father. "I wish this junk made more sense."

What he needed was a trained detective to help him sort through all the information his father had left behind. But Max couldn't ask anyone to help.

"This is a solo job," he said to himself. "And time is running out, Bollinger. The cops are going to start smelling a rat very soon."

With luck, he could keep Detective Malone's thoughts busy elsewhere, Max thought. Oh, he could try to get rid of her completely, but he was loath to do that. He intended to enjoy the chore of sidetracking her immensely. But he suspected that she couldn't be distracted for long—not even by sex.

Sheila drove back to the precinct house in a fine temper. Muttering to herself, she came up with lots of smart replies to Max's suggestion that they go to bed together. She should have rejected him flat. Caving in like a hormone-crazed teenager had been absolutely the wrong move.

But she hadn't been able to fight the feelings the man stirred in her. Did he have to be so physically attractive? So quick on the mental uptake? Such a smart mouth? He was everything Sheila appreciated in a man—even down to his talents as a great kisser.

Just thinking about his terrific kissing put Sheila in a foul mood.

"What's the matter with you?" Cowboy asked as they went off duty.

"Shut up."

"How many times have I told you what a sweet-talker you are, Malone?"

Sheila sighed. "Sorry. Rotten night. I need a day off, I guess."

Cowboy fumbled in his raincoat pocket for a book of matches. "Lucky for you, Piccolo had to switch schedules. I kindly gave him your Friday and Saturday for his Sunday, Monday and Tuesday."

Sheila blew up. "Who died and put you in charge of my life? Maybe I had plans for Friday! Did you consider that?"

"Nope," said Cowboy, lighting his cigar. "Enjoy your time off, Malone. See you Wednesday."

Sheila spent Sunday alternately studying and watching old Fred Astaire movies on public television. As the hours passed, her good intentions began to waver and eventually she gave up on the law books entirely and plunked herself in front of the television. It was amazing, she decided, how much Max Bollinger was like Fred.

Oh, Max was bigger, brawnier and a lot less graceful than the timeless Astaire, but there was something—some element—that they seemed to share. It was class, Sheila decided after watching *Royal Wedding*. Max Bollinger and Fred Astaire could dress themselves in tattered jeans and sweatshirts and still look like princes.

Before the next movie reached its romantic climax, Sheila put on her running shoes and went outside for some exercise. After a four-mile run, she came home and soaked in the tub for half an hour. Only when her thoughts meandered back to Max Bollinger did she climb out of the bath. She dried herself roughly, pulled on the football shirt she used as pajamas, and crawled into bed with a book that tried to teach her something about legal torts. She fell asleep and had a dream about making love with Max Bollinger in a courtroom.

On Monday night Sheila skipped her class at the law school. Instead, she put on a skirt and a pair of boots, the only silk blouse she owned, and topped it off with her "church" coat. Then she walked down the hill from her apartment toward the funeral home on Carson Street.

When she reached the right corner, she stopped. Alone, she stood beside a mailbox for a long time, watching the entrance of the funeral home. She knew tonight was the ceremony for the young man she'd killed in the park.

Muttering to herself, she said, "What am I doing here?"

She wasn't sure. Cowboy would throw a fit if he knew she'd come this far. But Sheila couldn't stop herself. Oddly enough, she wanted to go inside and speak to the rapist's family. Would they yell at her? Throw stones? For a time, she fantasized that they'd knock her down and scream at her—a grief-stricken family punishing their boy's killer.

But standing outside was as close as she could get. An invisible wall prevented Sheila from going any farther. For half an hour, she hung around watching the door, unable to make herself walk up the steps and go inside.

Around seven-thirty, an older woman in a belted raincoat scurried past Sheila, heading for the stone steps of the funeral home. Sheila caught a glimpse of the woman's face—a heavily lined face elaborately made up to hide the wrinkles and framed by a wiry halo of dyed red hair. She glanced once at Sheila and kept going. Her expression was outwardly blank—but in that split second, Sheila thought she saw something else: resignation, perhaps; a certain deadness in her eyes. Sheila's breath seemed to get stuck in her chest, for she was sure the woman was the victim's mother.

Sheila almost called out to her. But the words didn't come. The expression in the older woman's eyes had stopped her. It was as if the mother had expected her son to come to such a violent end. Sheila watched her struggle to open the heavy door, then disappear inside the building.

Nobody else went into the funeral home, and Sheila wondered if the young man's death was being mourned by no one but his mother—a mother who didn't seem surprised that her son had died during the commission of a crime.

What did it mean?

A car suddenly pulled up next to the curb and stopped. Blindly Sheila turned to hurry away, thinking for an instant that the car was carrying more mourners. But the passenger door opened, blocking her escape.

From inside the car, Max Bollinger's voice said, "Get in, Sheila."

She rocked to a stop, feeling absurdly guilty at having been caught in front of the funeral home. A hot blush rushed into her face.

Max leaned across the seat to look up at her from inside the low slung car. His expression was serious, his eyes keen in the darkness. He put out his hand. "Come on. If you're not going inside, I'll take you home."

Sheila swallowed hard. "Are you just passing by? Or have you been spying on me?"

"I've been parked across the street for the last half hour, as a matter of fact. I had a hunch you'd try something like this."

Humiliated, Sheila was tempted to spin around and walk home by herself. But the weather spoiled that plan just then, because the clouds suddenly opened and let out a spattering of cold rain. She hunched in her coat, still thinking of escape despite the needles of rain striking her face.

Sounding impatient, Max said, "For God's sake, get in. There's no sense in both of us freezing to death."

The wind whipped her hair around her head, blinding Sheila for a second and giving her a chance to compose her expression before he saw where her thoughts had been. He was right—she was freezing, and there was no sense hanging around on an empty street corner all night.

Making up her mind, Sheila climbed into the car and closed the door. She immediately found herself surrounded by luxury. The leather seats, the gleaming dashboard, the rumbling purr of a fine-tuned British engine all looked very expensive. The car's interior smelled vaguely of leather, polish and a scent that she recognized as Max—clean and masculine. On closer inspection, she noted that the leather seats were worn and the dashboard had a few burned-out lights, but the effect was still there. Max's car was like him—a class act.

He didn't put the Jaguar in gear yet, but sat half turned toward her and said, "You're an idiot, you know. What did you expect to gain by coming here tonight?"

His voice wasn't angry, just gently rebuking. The gentleness forced a lump into Sheila's throat—a lump so big she couldn't answer.

He continued, "You shouldn't have come."

"I— I couldn't stay away."

He reached over and brushed a trickle of rainwater from Sheila's cheek. At least she hoped it was rainwater. Max's touch was a gentle caress. "It's okay," he murmured. "You want to go home now?"

Sheila nodded and sat huddled in her coat while he pulled out into the street and drove slowly past the funeral home. She took one last look at the place through the rain-streaked window, then determinedly focused her attention on the road ahead and tried to pull herself together. Her heart was beating like mad.

Why did he have to turn up tonight, of all nights? She wasn't sure she had the strength to resist him.

"What's your address?"

She cleared her throat before trusting her voice. "It's three blocks up the hill. Take a right at this light."

Max obeyed, driving carefully. Sheila stole a look at him, and by the light from the dashboard saw that he was dressed in a suit and tie under his cashmere coat. He looked like a bank director or some kind of pricey doctor.

"You're dressed to kill," she remarked, mustering some of her usual spark. "Where have you been today?"

"You're referring to the suit? I put it on in case I had to go after you."

"What?"

"I figured you'd be the type to try a stunt like going to the kid's funeral, so I checked the newspaper to see what time you might be here. Lucky for both of us, you chickened out. I'm not good at funerals."

"I never chicken out!"

"Okay, bad choice of words. You got smart. Anyway, I watched to make sure you didn't do something crazy." He shot a glance across at her. "What *were* you doing, Sheila? Hoping to get some kind of punishment for what you did?"

Sheila sighed and rested her head back against the soft leather seat. "Maybe." She closed her eyes and let the car whisk her homeward. "I don't know for sure. I'm not thinking straight these days."

More to himself than to her, Max murmured, "That makes two of us."

Sheila's eyes snapped open. "What were you hoping to accomplish?" she demanded. "Did you think you'd catch me in a weak moment? Were you hoping to get lucky?"

He gave a short laugh. "I can't imagine you in a weak moment, Detective Malone."

"Damn straight."

"So I guess we'll just have to say that I was worried about you."

"I have a father who worries plenty, so don't feel obligated to help him out."

"Believe me, obligation isn't the reason I'm out on a rainy night looking for you."

"Then why?"

"Lord, you're a pistol, aren't you? Haven't you figured it out yet? Let's just say I feel we left some unfinished business when we parted Saturday night."

"You could have called the precinct house if you had anything to say about the Pletheridge break-in."

"I'm not talking about police business. I'm talking about man-to-woman business. Are you this dense all the time? Or is it some kind of act cops are taught at the police academy?"

"I am not dense. I just don't see what we've got in common. I—"

"We haven't got a damn thing in common!" Max burst out. "Believe me, you're very different from the women I normally meet. That's what's so blasted—I mean—"

"Watch it, Max. You're about to insult me."

"On the contrary," he said at once. "I'm about to insult myself. I've been obsessed with other aspects of my life for so long that I'd almost forgotten what it was like to be infatuated with a woman."

"Infatuated," Sheila repeated derisively. "The word even sounds like a guy with a fat head. Is that what you are?"

"I can't get you *out* of my head. Maybe that qualifies as stupidly obsessed. What's the matter? Haven't you ever had a man infatuated with you before?"

"Nope."

"I don't believe that. You're a beautiful woman, Sheila. You must have been just as beautiful when you were in school."

"In school I was a tall, skinny kid with a big mouth, and when I filled out and all the guys finally grew up taller than me I still had the big mouth, so I'm not exactly considered a good catch by my family. Most everybody figures I'm going to end up some kind of weird, gun-toting spinster."

"You must have had a few love affairs to convince them otherwise. A woman doesn't kiss the way you kissed me without a little practice."

"Oh, I slipped out of the convent now and then."

Max looked startled. "The convent?"

"That was a joke, dope. Mind you, I went to a good Catholic school run by the Sisters of Perpetual Guilt, but it wasn't actually a convent."

"So you had boyfriends?"

"Sure, I dated. When I went to the community college I saw a few guys, too, but I was still living at home with a houseful of brothers and one very vigilant father, so I wasn't exactly free to do as I pleased."

"And now?"

"What about now?"

"Are you seeing anyone?"

Sheila considered lying, but didn't for some reason she couldn't figure out. "No."

"Good," said Max. "Me neither. That makes it easy, at least."

"Makes *what* easy? I'd like to have one easy thing in my life right now, but— Wait, what about Elke?"

"What about her? She's a business associate."

"She's gorgeous."

Max smiled. "She's also engaged to a close friend of mine. They're getting married this summer. I'm supposed to fly back to Germany to be his best man. I told you, there's nothing romantic or sexual between me and Elke. We're friends."

Sheila couldn't imagine any woman being friends with Max Bollinger without noticing his sexual attractiveness, but she decided it would be imprudent to say so just then. She pointed out the windshield. "I live here. Pull over next to the hydrant."

Max did as she asked, slipping the Jaguar smoothly against the curb. He shut off the engine, but didn't move to get out of the car. Instead, he turned sideways and looked at her in the light that slanted down from a lamppost.

His gaze roved appreciatively down the silk edge of the blouse that peeked out from the neck of her coat, seemed to linger over the barely perceptible rise of her breasts, then slid past her skirt to the boots that covered her legs from her knees to the tips of her toes. Sheila felt as if his look warmed each of the places he noticed. She clamped her legs together, thus hoping to suppress her feelings.

He remarked, "You manage to keep yourself damnably well covered up when you're not pretending to be a hooker, don't you?"

"It's a cold night, in case you didn't notice."

"It's more than that with you, though, isn't it?"

"I'm not a spiffy dresser like Elke, if that's what you mean. Not on a cop's pay."

"Somehow I can't imagine you wearing strapless dresses and diamonds, anyway. I meant what I said before. You're different, Sheila. Warmer somehow."

Sheila found that her throat was suddenly very dry. The quiet intimacy of the car made her feel nervous. She could have touched Max if she dared to move her hand six inches, but she was afraid to make contact, even accidentally. She wasn't afraid of him, exactly, but of what might happen.

"Uh—I— I appreciate you bringing me home like this," she told him uncertainly. "It would have been a long walk in the rain. And thanks very much for—for—"

Max waited, his dark brows raised questioningly.

Sheila finished, "Thanks for not making a big deal out of what I did."

"Trying to go to the kid's funeral, you mean?"

"Yes. I— My partner would have jumped down my throat."

"He's concerned about you."

Sheila took a cautious look at Max. "He thinks I'm losing my marbles."

He smiled a little. "What do *you* think?"

Sheila took a deep breath. She *was* losing her marbles— at least where Max was concerned. Sitting just inches from him, she was suddenly as breathless as a girl at her first prom.

"I'll be okay," she assured him.

"I think so, too," Max replied, watching her face.

The moment stretched out and didn't snap until another car drove past, splashing a puddle against Max's window. That broke the spell, so he opened his door and came around the car with his black coat flying open in the wind.

Wordlessly, he helped her out of the passenger seat. His hand felt warm and firm around hers, and Sheila was slow to release it. She couldn't look Max in the eye as she started for the porch steps, but felt him place his hand on her lower back to guide her across the slippery sidewalk. It was a comforting touch—but surprisingly sexy, too. Her knees felt weak.

Sheila lived on the second floor of a small row house that was owned by one of her relatives. It was a modest place with peeling paint and a distinct sag in the porch floor, but the rent was low and Sheila liked its proximity to most neighborhood amenities. With Max standing just behind her, though, all the shortcomings of her home seemed even more apparent than ever.

Sheila's great-aunt Ellie lived on the first floor, but all the lights were out, indicating that Aunt Ellie had gone to bed early again. Still, Sheila felt enormously self-conscious as Max accompanied her to the door that led to her apartment.

She fumbled in her coat pocket for the key, turning into Max's path to give him the idea that he was definitely not going to be invited in. But Max automatically reached for her shoulders and suddenly they were standing toe to toe and looking at each other as if hypnotized.

"Max," she started, then found she couldn't finish.

He whispered her name in return and lowered his head until their lips were merely centimeters apart. A heartbeat passed before Sheila's hands moved unbidden through his open coat to the front of his shirt. Her touch signaled permission, and Max took her mouth with his. Sheila's brain went deliciously blank, and she leaned against him.

His lips urged hers to part and seconds later Max was kissing her senseless. Maybe it was the tension of the night—her aborted trip to the funeral home and the emotions that had fought inside her while she'd stood there alone in the darkness—but suddenly Sheila couldn't hold herself in check any longer. She pressed against his lean frame, snuggling her breasts against his chest and reveling in the sensation of his belly against hers, his hard thighs making erotic contact with her own, and his hands roving sensually down her back. As if some other woman had suddenly awakened inside her, she began to kiss him back for all she was worth.

Max unbuttoned her coat with one hand and slipped it inside, making contact with her silk blouse and the sensitive flesh beneath. As his lips traced a path down the tender length of her neck, he caressed her ribs one by one until Sheila sighed with desire. A soft moan escaped her lips just as he cupped her breast through the fabric of her blouse and bra. He bent to take her mouth again, savoring the moment she surrendered to his touch.

I'm lost, Sheila thought. *I'm going to give in.*

Four

In a deep recess of his brain, Max could still think, but he wasn't sure how much longer that was going to last. The woman in his arms was too tantalizing. She was wonderful. He wanted to snatch her into his arms and carry her up the stairs to her bed.

Her breast felt small and warm in his hand—soft and feminine. Her mouth tasted hungry, and the quiet sound he heard from her throat made his heart beat faster. Without thinking, he unfastened the top buttons of her blouse, needing to feel her bare flesh against his. When he found her nipple with his fingertips, Sheila moved convulsively, as if desire had suddenly flared inside her. She gasped. He kissed her face and earlobe, then pressed a series of hot, moist kisses down her long, lovely throat.

She whispered his name—first passionately, then with more force when she seemed to realize what he wanted to do. He arched her backward with one arm and bent down to take her breast with his lips, but Sheila twisted away, breathing erratically. Her green eyes were wide and full of conflicting emotions.

"Wait," she gasped, catching a handful of the hair at the back of his head. "Don't."

"You're as turned on as I am, Sheila."

"I can't make love right here," she said, pulling her blouse together with one hand and unconsciously caressing the back of his neck with the other. "*Please.* Half my family lives on this block. I can't—"

"Let's go upstairs."

She laughed unsteadily. "Then they'll all start telephoning! You don't understand. They're all *watching*."

As if to prove her point, the porch light suddenly came on, nearly blinding both of them. Max couldn't help laughing as he held on to her. "Why do I feel like a teenager again? Is your father going to come out with a shotgun?"

She shook her head, smiling oddly. "No, he lives a few blocks away. It's my aunt Ellie and aunt Mary and grandmother Malone and—"

"You're not kidding?" Max demanded, taking a quick glance around at the house across the street and on either side. "We've really got an audience?"

"I'm sure of it," replied Sheila, sounding more composed by the second. "They're all very protective of me."

"Shall we give them a little excitement?"

"Max—"

He silenced her with another kiss—one that sent his own hormones into another kamikaze dive. Sheila responded, too, her slender hands playing delicately at the back of his neck and at the most ticklish spot on his chest. Max groaned, unable to stop himself from becoming thoroughly aroused. Her body felt wonderful against his—slim and strong and full of promise. The contact made him hungry for more, and he moved against her, making no secret about what he wanted.

For a few seconds, Sheila moved rhythmically with him. Then common sense took over, and she pushed against his chest.

She couldn't look him in the eye, and he thought he could see a faint blush of sexual excitement in her cheeks. Her mouth trembled when she tried to smile and couldn't manage it.

"Look," she said, apparently deciding to go for honesty. "I don't know where my head is, but it's not where it's supposed to be."

"Maybe it's time to let your head take a vacation."

"I can't. This would never work, anyway, Max."

"Why not?" He tightened his hold on her. "You can't deny that we're hot for each other."

"That doesn't make it right. Hell, I'm all screwed up! I need to get my act together. And you— Well, you belong with someone else, anyway."

"What the hell are you talking about?"

"Look around," she advised, pulling out of his embrace and hugging her coat around herself. "Does this neighborhood look like home to you?"

"No, but—"

"You come from another world, don't you see?"

"Sheila, for God's sake—"

"I'm a *cop*," she said, her voice suddenly cracking. "I'm not cut out to play Cinderella, understand? Go find a nice girl at the country club, Slick. Guys like you don't belong with girls like me."

She left him standing on the porch then. With one last, vivid look over her shoulder, she unlocked her door and slipped inside. A moment later, he heard her footsteps hurrying up the wooden stairs.

Max went down the porch steps, his head swimming. One minute he'd been making love to a beautiful woman, and now he was standing in the rain. Where the hell had he gone wrong?

She'd been upset. The funeral thing had caused her more turmoil than she'd let on. He should have known better than to push her tonight.

Rethinking his strategy, Max drove himself home.

Sheila slammed into her apartment, feeling ready to cry and scream at the same time. What the hell had she been thinking of? She tore off her clothes and threw them into a heap on the floor. Naked, she climbed into bed and lay there trying not to think. The cool sheets quickly warmed up and soon felt erotically smooth against her bare skin. When she realized her brain had started to work again, she was dreaming about Max and imagining all the places his wonderful hands could go.

In the morning after a long and restless night, Sheila crawled out of bed and stood in front of the mirror that hung on her bathroom door. Examining her reflection, she decided she'd been looking lousy lately. She'd lost a few pounds and her hair had gotten too long, and she couldn't remember the last time she'd used makeup except to slather it on to go out on decoy detail. Her wardrobe was sadly in need of an update, too. A full-time job and law school were taking their toll.

Most of all, however, she couldn't seem to forget how lovely Elke had looked at the opera. Sheila had felt like a mutt from the dog pound compared to Elke's sleek beauty. Surely Max had been lying when he'd called *her* beautiful.

On impulse, Sheila decided to go shopping. It might get her mind off Max and back where it belonged.

She dressed quickly and headed down to Carson Street on foot, enjoying the sunshine after a long weekend of sleet and snow. It was a beautiful day, and the whole neighborhood seemed to be outside taking advantage of the break in the weather. Housewives with baby strollers clogged the sidewalks, while delivery trucks made a mess of traffic by double-parking up and down the streets. A straggly line of kindergarten students—all holding hands and looked delighted to be out of their classroom—dutifully followed their teacher up the steps of the post office.

Sheila stopped to grab a cup of espresso and a Danish at Hedland's Coffee Shop on the corner. Sitting at the counter, she had a long flirtation with Olaf Hedland, the sixty-five-year-old proprietor of the landmark restaurant. Cheered, she continued up the street, going into the shoe store to say hello to Mrs. O'Malley and buying a couple of newspapers from the Wongs' newsstand on Seventh Street. She waved at two cops sitting in a cruiser at the corner, and they waved back, rolling down the windows and calling "good mornings" to her.

At last she reached her destination—a tiny dress shop tucked between Libretto's Gift Shop and a travel agency. The shop was owned by Mrs. Elvira Ephron, an elderly woman who still dyed her hair a fiery red and wore her fingernails as long as a mandarin prince's. The shop was feminine in the extreme—chintz-covered chairs, fresh flowers, the scent of violets in the air, rhapsodic music filtering from somewhere behind the scenes, and racks and racks of lovely clothes. Mrs. Ephron favored lace and satin and colors like pink and lavender for herself, but she managed to bring truly unique and stylish clothes to the neighborhood women.

"Sheila Kathleen!" Mrs. Ephron cried when the bell on the door to her shop tinkled and Sheila stepped onto the powder-blue rug. "Merciful heaven, is that you?"

Smiling shyly, Sheila advanced on the old woman who was busily consulting the horoscopes in a glossy magazine. She was glad to see that Mrs. Ephron hadn't changed in the few years since Sheila had last been in the store. Still the same carefully applied makeup, the pretty flowered dress with a utilitarian apron tied in front, the pincushion efficiently attached to her plump wrist. Mrs. Ephron had been a widow for three decades, and she'd built her business with her own hands—buying clothes, selling them herself, making meticulous alterations and plying her customers with herbal tea while they waited for their purchases to be wrapped.

Mrs. Ephron whipped off her bifocals and gave Sheila's jeans and bulky sweater a frosty once-over.

"Goodness!" she declared. "What cat dragged you down the street?"

"I look terrible, huh?"

Tiny Mrs. Ephron leaped to her feet and hugged Sheila fondly. "On the contrary, my dear. You simply look a little disheveled. That's in style, I'm sure, but I never could understand the popularity of that look. What man wants a woman looking like she just popped out of bed?"

Sheila laughed. "You'd be surprised, I bet!"

Mrs. Ephron smiled slyly. "I'm not from the Dark Ages, my girl. *You* might be surprised. What can I do for you today?"

Sheila gave up trying to explain her feelings and simply sighed. "Everything!"

Her eyes sparkling, the proprietress asked, "Do you mean that? I've been waiting years to get my hands on you, you know."

Laughing, Sheila said, "You have?"

"Of course! You have your father's wonderful bone structure, your grandmother's wonderful chin, but your dear mother—God rest her soul—never had a figure as marvelous as yours."

That odd lump was forming in Sheila's throat again. "I just don't feel like a woman anymore, Mrs. E. I'm tired of jeans and boots. I'd like to feel—well—feminine again."

Mrs. Ephron's watery blue eyes were sharp. "What's troubling you, my dear?"

"It's nothing," Sheila replied quickly, glad that Mrs. Ephron didn't read the newspapers. "I need a change, that's all."

The old woman's face shone with a smile. "Well, then, let's get to work! What are you shopping for? A nice dress, maybe? A beautiful, sexy sweater?"

"I could use something for a party. My dad's annual Saint Patrick's Day bash is Thursday night. I was hoping—"

Mrs. Ephron linked her arm with Sheila's and hurried her to the racks at the back of the store. "I have some ideas already. You need something dramatic and wonderful in a vibrant color!"

"Anything but green," Sheila interjected. "No sensible Irishman wears green on Saint Paddy's Day—at least not in my dad's bar."

Mrs. Ephron's ring-clad fingers flew expertly over the many dresses and party outfits that hung on their padded hangers. She thrust one after another against Sheila to have a look at them, but shook her head each time and put the dress back again. "These will never do. Too frilly! Your personality requires something more exciting. Do you still have that awful job, my dear?"

Bemused, Sheila admitted, "I'm still a cop."

"What your grandmother Kincannon would say to that! Tch, tch!"

"I'm going to law school now."

"Are you, darling? That's wonderful! I can imagine you in practice in a lovely office downtown and meeting handsome young judges for romantic lunches. Come to me for a good gray suit when the time comes—nothing mannish, of course, but soft and elegant. Ah, try this! And this one, too!"

As Sheila accepted one dress after another, she began to feel better. Coming to see Mrs. Ephron was exactly the tonic she had needed. Sheila had happy memories of the shop. When she'd been growing up, she had come along each time her mother needed a one-of-a-kind dress for some special occasion or other. Sheila had come herself for a graduation dress, too. And how many times had Sheila and her teenage girlfriends hung around outside the windows, exclaiming over the glamorous mannequins Mrs. Ephron re-dressed every Saturday morning?

The doorbell jingled again, bringing both Sheila and Mrs. Ephron laughingly back to their senses.

"Let me try these on," Sheila said, barely able to hold on to the pile of pretty things over her arm. "You take care of your other customer."

"Don't spoil my fun, now," Mrs. Ephron trilled over her shoulder, fluttering to the front of the store. "I want to see you model each one of these!"

Feeling almost jaunty for the first time in nearly a week, Sheila took the clothing to the curtained dressing room and stripped off her jeans and sweater. She hummed along with the music as she made her selection among the many items Mrs. Ephron had chosen. Her eye was immediately caught by a wine-colored outfit—a jumpsuit made of the finest soft challis. Impulsively, she tried it on first.

The jumpsuit looked so good that Sheila was startled by her reflection. She actually looked pretty. The jumpsuit clung to her slim hips and refined her waist to a sensuous curve. The deep red shade heightened the bright color of her auburn hair and intensified her cameo-pale skin. She shook out her hair until it was boldly tumbled around her face, then stood back to study the results.

Sheila was surprised by the haunted look lurking in her eyes as she gazed at her reflection in the dressing-room mirror. But the outfit looked wonderful—snappy and sexy with a subtle fit and a warm, touchable color. She knew she didn't need to look further for the right outfit to wear to her father's party. In it, she felt wonderfully attractive again.

"Sheila!" Mrs. Ephron called gaily from the front of the shop. "Let's see what you've got on!"

Barefoot, Sheila stepped out into the shop to show Mrs. Ephron the jumpsuit. "This isn't bad," she started, heading toward the chintz chair where Mrs. Ephron sat. "I—"

Then Sheila faltered, recognizing the person who was calmly sitting in the other chintz chair with a cup of tea balanced gracefully on his knee and a look on his handsome face that showed how pleased he was with himself.

"Max!" Sheila growled from between clenched teeth.

"You're right," Max said pleasantly, appreciatively studying her outfit. "It's not bad at all, Sheila. In fact, it's quite stunning."

"What are you doing here?"

"He came to see you, my dear," Mrs. Ephron cooed, sounding pleased as punch to be entertaining such an attractive specimen as Max Bollinger. "We're just getting to know each other, dear." The elderly woman positively giggled. "And I believe Mr. Bollinger might be smitten, Sheila."

"Is he, indeed?" Sheila asked coldly.

"Indeed," Max agreed, lazing to his feet at last to get a better look at her outfit. "And if you start dressing like that all the time, Detective, you're going to find me following you wherever you go."

"Isn't that what you're doing?" she snapped, then whirled around and stormed back toward the dressing room.

"Sheila," Max called on a laugh. "Wait—"

Mrs. Ephron squealed as he hurriedly thrust his cup into her hands and went after Sheila with long, quick strides.

"Really, Mr. Bollinger, you shouldn't go back there," bleated Mrs. Ephron. "Oh, dear, oh, *dear*!"

Max caught up with her at the doorway of the dressing room and took hold of her arm. "Sheila, wait! I didn't mean to make you shy."

"I am not shy!" She spun around and glared up into Max's handsome face—the same face she'd dreamed about last night. "I'm disgusted! You have no right tailing me like this!"

"I can't resist. I saw you come in here, and— Lord, do you know how gorgeous you look in this thing?"

With a wicked smile, he wrapped his arm around her waist and forced Sheila back into the dressing room. They could hear Mrs. Ephron making helpless little cries at the front of the store, but Max took no notice. Sheila managed to grab his shoulders before she lost her balance completely.

"Max, let me go!"

"I've always wanted to see the inside of a ladies' dressing room. It's been a fantasy of mine. Have they got some sexy underwear you could try on? Those things with garters and—"

"You couldn't pay me enough to try on *anything* for you, buster!"

Max seemed unaware of her struggles as he pulled Sheila down onto the plush velour chair in the corner of the dressing room. As clumsy as a couple of anxious adolescents, they groped for an instant, Sheila still halfheartedly trying to escape, Max seeking to hold her back.

"Hush," he told her, "before Mrs. Ephron thinks we're doing something naughty."

"She *already* thinks we're doing something naughty! Max—"

His mouth covered hers, his hands roaming down her body until the right combination of body parts matched and held. He molded her hip, played a caress up the curve of her waist and was just about to take possession of her breast when Sheila blocked his progress and wrenched her mouth away from his.

"Stop it!"

He was smiling, his dark eyes agleam. "You could get out of my lap whenever you like, Detective. You must be trained in all kinds of self-defense."

With her nose less than an inch from his, she retorted, "I don't want to break any of your bones."

"I'm surprisingly resilient. Go ahead and try anything you want."

"You'd like that, wouldn't you?"

"Very much. I find this place highly erotic, don't you?" With his eyes heavy lidded, he traced a soft pattern on her hip. "Imagine all the women who've undressed in this room, all the nightgowns they've tried on, the dresses—"

"The thought of women undressing doesn't do anything to my libido," Sheila interrupted tartly, trying unsuccessfully to disentangle her long legs from his.

"But it sends my libido through the roof," Max replied, stilling her legs and capturing her mouth once more. He groaned as their lips met and he cupped her head between his hands to make the kiss more perfect. Deftly, he managed to bend Sheila back over the arm of the chair and slide her sideways so she was pinned there. His hard thigh slipped between her legs, making Sheila fully aware of his aroused state. He pulled away to give her one raking stare that spelled pure desire. Then he kissed her again, his hand trailing to the neckline of the jumpsuit. He feathered a wispy touch on the skin above her breast. Sheila's determination to fend him off began to wilt. His tongue was too erotic against hers. When he nibbled at her throat, she found herself weakening further. He nipped her earlobe, and the tiny pain set off a chain reaction of erotic explosions. Sheila tingled all over—every nerve-ending alive with passion.

Her slid the jumpsuit over her shoulder and realized that she wasn't wearing a bra. With a growl of pleasure, he kissed her shoulder, his tongue trailing a hot, wet line across her collarbone.

"Max, Mrs. Ephron will be horrified!"

"I can hear her giggling," Max murmured, his lips busy pressing kisses to the soft skin above Sheila's right breast. "If we stay here an hour, she'll have something to gossip about for years."

Sheila gasped as Max's hand found her left breast and coaxed her nipple erect. "I don't want to be a subject of gossip!"

"Relax," coaxed Max, maneuvering her over the edge of the chair. "It'll be fun."

They hit the carpet with a thud that drove all the breath from Sheila's body. Max landed on top, his legs forcing hers apart. Sheila tensed to fight him, but at that moment Max must have sensed her consternation. He seized her around the waist and rolled, managing to put Sheila above him. She sat up abruptly, but found herself in an exceedingly sexual position astride Max's horizontal frame. She blushed hotly and pushed her tangled hair off her face.

"You're crazy!" she cried.

"Shh." He planted his fingertips across her lips. "Be a little quiet, will you?"

"You're crazy," she repeated, only slightly more quietly than before. "Do you know what you're doing?"

"I know what I'd like to be doing." Max's smile was sexy and knowing as he traced the shape of her mouth and chin. "I dreamed about you all night, Sheila."

She pushed his hand away, not wanting to admit that the same fate had befallen her, too. "You should learn to be satisfied with your dreams."

"Not when the real thing could be even more exciting. How does this thing come off, anyway?" Max tugged the jumpsuit down from both her shoulders. "If we were quick, Mrs. Ephron would never guess—"

"How dumb do you think she is?" Sheila exploded. "How dumb do you think *I* am?" She rolled off Max and sat on the floor beside him. "You're not what I expected at all, Slick."

He grinned and linked his hands behind his head, staying comfortable on the floor. "What did you expect?"

"From a classy guy like you—a little more subtlety, at least."

"Subtle is good," Max agreed. "But it's slow. And I want you too much to proceed slowly."

"Then you don't understand women."

"I think I understand you," he countered. "I can see you're attracted to me, Sheila. Why waste time?"

"Maybe because I don't trust you yet."

Max propped himself on one elbow. "Look, Sheila, there's something simmering between us that doesn't happen very often. Why are you so reluctant to recognize it?"

Five

———

Trying to look indignant, Sheila snatched up her clothes and headed out into the shop in search of Mrs. Ephron—still wearing the jumpsuit. She was damned if she'd take it off with Max roaming freely around the dressing rooms.

Damn, I wish I knew how to handle him! she said to herself in desperation. He had a bewildering effect on her that she seemed incapable of resisting. She struggled into her boots, leaning precariously on the counter.

He followed her after he'd composed himself, but when he arrived at the cash register, Sheila noticed that Mrs. Ephron was nowhere to be found. A note lay on the counter. "Leave the key under the doormat."

"Where could she have gone?" Sheila asked, impatient to leave the store and Max far behind. She yanked her boot with such force that she had to clutch the counter to keep from falling.

Max flipped the sign that dangled on the front door. It was prettily decorated with little purple flowers and read, Be Back In One Hour.

He gave Sheila a bemused smile. "Looks like Mrs. Ephron has given us the run of the shop."

Mortified, Sheila hobbled past Max to look at the sign herself. "Good grief! What did she think we were doing?"

Max lounged against the counter, laughing. "No doubt she assumed the worst. You blush beautifully, you know."

"This is not a joking matter, Max! My—my reputation hangs in the balance."

"I'm sure we only improved it." Max toyed with the jewelry hanging on display beside the cash register while watching her stamp her heel down so her foot settled into her boot properly. "Your reputation is pretty dull, I bet."

. "There's nothing wrong with dull! How am I going to pay for this if she's not here?"

Max unlooped a long string of pearls from the display. Catching Sheila's hand, he drew her closer and turned her around, making a soothing sound when she tried to pull away. Playfully he wound the pearls around her neck and then admired how they nestled between her breasts in the low-cut jumpsuit. "Perfect," he said, brushing her hair off her shoulders to get a better view.

"Don't play games with me, please."

"Just because we're grown-up, doesn't mean we can't play games."

"Your games are dangerous."

"I have one in mind right now."

Sheila was having trouble breathing. The pearls tickled her skin and were making her nipples stand out against the fabric of the jumpsuit, but she couldn't stop herself from asking, "What is it?"

He used the pearls to draw circles on her skin. "We have this whole shop to ourselves for an hour. It's like a Victorian lady's paradise, isn't it?"

"A—a little."

Against her ear he whispered, "I want to undress you, Sheila. Then watch you try on everything in the store."

Her voice squeaked. "Everything?"

"Well, I could pick out a few items since we're limited to just an hour. I'll bet Mrs. Ephron keeps the lacy stuff under the counter, doesn't she?"

Not under the counter, Sheila knew. But in the drawers of a special antique armoire. The drawers were full of lace camisoles and satin chemises—sexy, feminine, desirable wisps of nothing.

"What do you say?" Max asked huskily, following the trail of the pearls across her bare shoulder with his lips. "Will you play with me?"

Sheila was sure he could hear her heart beating, for the blood roared in her ears and made her limbs tremble. Max's mouth left her skin both hot and shivery. The pearls felt sensuous against her flesh. The idea of trying on lace and satin, letting Max watch as she fastened every hook and adjusted every strap, was highly erotic.

But she had one tiny iota of common sense left, and after a moment, she steeled herself to say no to his proposal.

Twisting out of his range, she said breathlessly, "I can't."

"You won't, you mean."

"Either way, you're out of luck." Sheila reached for a pen that had been left near the cash register. A box of Mrs. Ephron's lavender notepaper was also handy, so Sheila began to scribble the shopkeeper a note. "I have to run," she told Max. "I have things to do."

He leaned on the counter. "Important things?"

"Yes. And I don't want you following me."

"Why would I—"

"You've been snooping, Slick, and I don't like it."

"Snooping! Listen, seeing you today was purely an accident."

"Tell it to the marines," she shot back.

"It's true. I was going into the brewery when I spotted you across the street. I called, but you were a thousand miles away, judging by the dreamy look on your face. What were you thinking about, anyway?"

"Ax murderers," she retorted, embarrassed that he'd caught her unawares. No doubt she'd been thinking about *him*.

He laughed. "I don't doubt it. Look, I'm sorry I surprised you. I couldn't resist. That's all. I followed you for a couple of blocks and when you ducked into this place, I went after you. Mrs. Ephron is a very nice lady. She likes you a lot."

"You were gossiping about me, is that it?"

"Does that upset you?"

Sheila finished her note and threw down the pen. "You have no business following me."

"Why not? Because of some ridiculous police policy? Or because of last night?"

Sheila decided to play dumb. "Last night?"

"Specifically the kissing part," said Max. "Are you upset because I kissed you?"

"Certainly not! I—"

"Good," he told her, "because suddenly I find myself wanting to do it again."

Sheila grabbed her clothes, snatched her coat off the chair where she'd left it and headed for the door. Max beat her there and held it open for her. Sheila stopped and looked at him. "You haven't figured it out yet, have you?

I don't want to spend time with you. I can't! My job is at stake. I'm a *cop*. I can't play any games with you, Max."

"Let's not pretend that it's your job that's keeping us apart," Max shot back. "You're afraid of me, Sheila, pure and simple."

"Afraid!" She laughed rudely and breezed out of the shop. "Are you kidding? Do you know what kind of risks I take practically every day I go to work?"

"I can guess," he replied, closing the door behind them and dropping the key under the mat. "But none of those risks involve the thing you're most afraid to lose."

"My life?" she asked, turning to face him.

"Control," Max answered. "You like to be in control, and you can't always manage that with me, Sheila. You're afraid something wild and dangerous is going to happen when we're together."

"I can never lose control," she declared. "Not ever. When a cop loses her grip, somebody could die. And I don't want that somebody to be me."

"You're not going to die in this situation," Max said, more softly this time. "In fact, I might actually be good for you, Sheila."

She glared at him and he stared back at her as if daring her to respond.

There was no time. In the next second, Sheila heard her name called from the street. She tore her gaze from Max's and saw a burly man making his way through the traffic.

"Honk all you like," he yelled at the driver of a red station wagon. "It won't make me walk any faster!"

Sheila groaned at the sight of him stomping across the street unmindful of the traffic light and speeding cars. "Dad, watch out!"

Beside her, Max muttered, "That's your father?"

"Behave yourself," she commanded under her breath. "I don't want him getting the wrong idea about us."

"I'll be the soul of discretion."

"Sheila!" bellowed Tommy Malone, stepping over the curb like a marauding bull. "Sheila Kathleen, why haven't you called in three days? What d'you expect me to be—a mind reader? Where have you been? And who's this?"

Tommy Malone was a big, hale Irishman, known for his generous heart, his Irish moods and his reputation as one of the city's most decorated cops on the force. Now retired, he ran a tavern with his brother Tipper in an old building on the busiest corner in the South Side. The two brothers, with their full white hair and their handsome faces, were popular with widows, little children and the hundreds of regular patrons of Malone's Tavern—everyone from millworkers and retired cops to upwardly mobile young professionals who parked their sports cars outside and brought their briefcases into the bar. Everybody loved the Malone brothers.

But Tommy Malone wasn't always popular with his own daughter—especially where her love life was concerned. Sheila saw the avid curiosity burning in her father's flushed face and knew she had to head him off quickly.

"This is nobody, Dad," Sheila said hastily. "A man I met, that's all."

Max wasn't going to let her get away with that. He drew himself up to his full height, looked Tommy Malone square in the eye and stuck out his hand for a shake. "I'm Max Bollinger, sir, and I'm delighted to meet you. Sheila has told me so much about you."

Sheila choked, but her father started to beam. "Has she, now? She's a good girl, my Sheila. Has she cooked you a decent meal yet, young man? She has her mother's recipe for stew, and it'll melt your heart, I swear!"

Tommy Malone's brogue seemed to thicken on special occasions, Sheila noted, particularly when there was someone to impress.

"Dad," she said firmly, "I'm not going to cook for Max. He's—"

"Newly back in town," Max interrupted. "I haven't had time to get to know everything about your lovely daughter yet, Mr. Malone."

"Where are you from, lad?"

"Originally from the city, but I've been away for several years on business."

"Oh?" Tommy Malone's sharp gaze took in Max's expensive leather jacket, his casual but obviously carefully selected clothes, and assumed that Max was an ideal catch for his daughter. "What business are you in?"

"He's a Bollinger, Dad," Sheila explained warily. "Of Bollinger's Brewery."

"Oho!" Tommy's face lit up. "Well, I'm pleased indeed to meet you, my lad. Pleased, indeed! Has Sheila invited you to our party Thursday night?"

"Dad—"

"She hasn't had time to mention it yet, sir."

"Well, you must come, of course. Saint Paddy's Day at Malone's Tavern—you'll come, I hope?"

Max was grinning to beat the band, and he slid his arm around Sheila's shoulder. "Wouldn't miss it, sir." He gave Sheila a squeeze.

Grinding her teeth, Sheila said, "You didn't have to do that, Dad."

"And why not? He's a good man, I can see that right away. He'll fit in nicely, I'm sure. Bring him before eight, please. We'll see that he gets some supper."

Tommy Malone spun around and set off down the street, whistling with pleasure and waving to anyone in the neighborhood who hailed him.

Thoroughly enraged, Sheila swung on Max. "Why did you have to go and accept that invitation?"

"How could I refuse? He's a charming man, Sheila. And now I know where you got your green eyes."

"*And* my hot temper!"

"We'll find a way to cool that down," Max promised.

"We will not! In case you haven't figured it out yet, Mr. Bollinger, I want nothing to do with you! The only time I intend to see you is in the line of duty. Otherwise—"

"Sheila—"

"Otherwise you are going to steer clear of me, understand? I don't want you following me around or calling me or showing up at my father's place—"

"It's a free world," Max said mildly.

"Not where I'm concerned!" Sheila retorted. "You and me—we're history!"

"I can't let that happen," argued Max. "I've always been attracted by women of mystery, and you're irresistible. I can't figure you out, Sheila. And I want to know everything about you. I want to know what makes you tick—how you think, how you laugh, how you make love. I want to know what makes you happy and sad. I want to—"

"Forget it," snapped Sheila. "Leave me alone, Max. I mean it!"

She hurried away from him, glancing only once over her shoulder to be sure he wasn't following. He wasn't. But he was standing in the middle of the sidewalk with the most infuriating grin on his face. Sheila wanted to throw something at him, but nothing was handy. She stormed home.

She couldn't get him out of her mind, of course. Every time she closed her eyes, she could see his cocky smile. And even with the television blaring in her apartment, she could almost hear Max's warm voice in her ear. It made her shiver.

She slept badly that night as a result of the tumult in her mind, and dragged herself to work fifteen minutes late. Even as she marched up the steps of the precinct house, she realized she was thinking about Max. She grumbled and cursed under her breath.

Cowboy looked up from his desk in the squad room and saw her coming. He got up before she threw her jacket and scarf on her desk.

"Come in here a minute," he said, gesturing into an empty interrogation room away from the other cops who were busy on the phone or talking with each other.

Sheila led the way, unwinding a long red scarf from around her neck. "What's going on?"

"I found something." Cowboy held a manila file folder aloft and closed the door after him. "I thought you might be interested."

Sheila sat on the edge of the scarred table and flipped open the folder. She frowned at the first few pages, unable to make sense of what she was looking at. "How about making this easier on me?"

Cowboy thrust his hands into the front pockets of his jeans and leaned back against the closed door. "Aren't we in a lousy mood this morning? Didn't you have a nice couple of days off?"

"Nice enough," Sheila replied cagily. "What's all this paperwork about?"

"A murder," Cowboy said, coming to his point. "Four years ago, a local loan shark by the name of Enrique Furmire disappeared. His family believed he'd died, and the police department agreed, even though the body was never found. Enrique was not a real popular guy, if you know what I mean.''

''All this happened before I joined the police force.''

''Me, too. In fact, five years ago, the department wasn't computerizing much of their records, which was part of the problem.''

''Problem?''

''After the Pletheridge break-in, I ran Max Bollinger's name into the computer and came up with nothing. But I mentioned Max's name to a couple of old cops I play cards with once in a while, and one of them remembered him.''

Thoroughly awake now, Sheila asked, ''What did he remember?''

Cowboy came to sit on the table beside Sheila and flipped through a few of the pages in the folder to show her something. ''Max Bollinger was one of the key suspects in the case of the missing loan shark. Half the police force believed Max killed the guy and disposed of the body.''

Sheila's heart gave a lurch. ''Are you kidding?''

''I'm not kidding. I found—''

''Max Bollinger has been out of the country for four years.''

''Exactly. He left immediately after the loan shark disappeared.''

Sheila felt as if she'd been stabbed in the chest. She could hardly breathe and her hands were suddenly shaking.

''Of course I can't prove anything,'' Cowboy went on, unaware of Sheila's state of mind as he took the file from her trembling hands and scanned the pages. ''The cops couldn't pin anything on Max at the time, and five years isn't going to make the clues any clearer, but—''

''You think *Max Bollinger* killed somebody?''

Cowboy looked at her, searching Sheila's face with a suddenly alert expression. "It's possible."

Sheila's throat tightened. "I don't believe it."

"Why do you say that?"

"I— I can't imagine that he's capable of it. That's all." Sheila struggled to control herself. "He's— I don't know, he doesn't seem like the type."

Cowboy grinned wryly. "Too charming? Too handsome? What's going on, Malone? Since when have you started being affected by a pretty face?"

"I'm not affected! He—he just seemed okay, that's all."

"He could be some kind of psycho for all we know!"

Sheila swallowed hard, averting her face so Cowboy couldn't guess what she was thinking. Had her attraction to Max blocked her cop's intuition? Even now, she found herself not thinking about the case, but about the man who'd kissed her. When she could control her voice again, she took a breath and asked, "Why was Max suspected in the first place?"

"Apparently his old man was into the loan shark for a lot of money. Enrique demanded payment, but old Bollinger couldn't come up with the scratch. Miraculously, Enrique disappeared and Bollinger was off the hook."

Sheila frowned, shaken by what Cowboy was telling her—and what she already knew was true. Max had explained his father's financial crisis, but had conveniently not mentioned any loan sharks.

"What are you thinking?" Cowboy asked curiously.

Sheila shook her head. "I don't know. I'm surprised, I guess. I have to admit there's something about Bollinger that makes me nervous, but I didn't— I have a hard time picturing him as a killer."

"He's had some time to clean up his act. Four years out of the country to avoid prosecution—"

"What are you going to do?" Sheila asked, already thinking about the next step. "Will you reopen the case?"

Cowboy tucked the papers back inside his folder. "I can't—not exactly. But you know I'd like to get a shot at Homicide. Maybe if I free-lance on this one, somebody downtown will notice me. I'm going to study the files. The Furmire murder is still technically in our jurisdiction. If any of this information looks like it might hook up with the Pletheridge break-in, I'll have to call the guys at the Third Precinct, I guess."

"You still think Max had something to do with the missing jewelry?"

"It's too much of a coincidence to believe he'd turn up on that particular night otherwise, don't you think?"

Sheila nodded slowly. "Okay. Let me know what you find."

"You're still interested in the case?"

Shrugging, Sheila tried to smile and said, "Why not? Everybody likes a good mystery."

As it turned out, Cowboy didn't learn anything new during the next couple of days. Sheila was busy responding to calls within the precinct, but she couldn't get Max Bollinger out of her head. Was he a murderer? If so, why couldn't she let some other cop worry about it? Why couldn't she forget about Max Bollinger the way she forgot half the people she met in the course of her work?

To top things off, she began to worry that he might try to see her again. A cop and a suspect? The combination was lethal.

To avoid contact with him—even so much as a single phone call—she took to spending less and less time at her apartment. When she wasn't on duty, she took her books to the college library and tried to study in a quiet corner where nobody knew her. She went home only to sleep and didn't rest well even when she did burrow in her bed. All she could think about was Max's kiss, the sensation of his strong body next to hers. Jamming her pillow over her head, she tried not to think about him, but she couldn't stop.

At work, she threw herself into every call, following up on two burglaries and helping Cowboy with a drug investigation he was running. She didn't want to relax—for fear Max might intrude on her thoughts even more frequently.

But Saint Patrick's Day at Malone's Tavern was a holiday observed the way most watering holes celebrated New Year's Eve. Every year, the bar was four deep with singing patrons, the tables were jammed with rollicking partygoers, and the music—a trio of Irish tenors—was barely loud enough to be heard over the roar of the crowd.

In the midst of all the activity, the Malone brothers held court. Tipper and Tommy, both former policemen, were the most popular of barkeepers. Their families were expected to be on hand, too.

Sheila was tempted to skip her father's annual Saint Patrick's Day bash, but decided at last that she'd never get away with it. Not going would be a signal for the whole family to start pestering her about what was wrong.

She wasted part of the evening, but around nine o'clock, she dressed herself in jeans and a sweater and boots. No way would she wear the sexy jumpsuit Max had helped pick out. Just looking at it reminded Sheila of their encounter in the shop—an incident she hoped to forget. As a concession to the occasion, Sheila brushed her red hair until it gleamed, and let it curl around her head and shoulders. Then she set off walking down the hill to Malone's Tavern. The night was cold but clear, and the front door of the tavern was so jammed with carousing patrons that she shunned it and slipped in through the kitchen.

Her aunt Mary and brother Larkin were sharing a bottle of beer and a couple of plates of stew when Sheila pushed through the door along with a chilly blast of March wind.

"Sheila, honey!" Larkin lazed to his feet, a tall, handsome drink of water with the Malone green eyes and a lock of unruly hair that fell across his broad forehead and gave his melancholy Irish face a dash of romance. He also had a lopsided smile that had broken many a heart in high school. He was just twenty-two and finishing his education at a nearby seminary. Larkin, it seemed, intended to become a priest. He bear-hugged his sister and gave her a sloppy kiss.

"Darlin'," he drawled in a put-on thick brogue, "you're lookin' as lovely as ever, in spite of that godawful sweater. Didn't that used to be Dad's?"

"He gave it to me," Sheila replied, not taking offense and giving her brother's cheek a fond tweak. "What are you doing here? Shouldn't you be studying in a monk's cell someplace?"

"I should, but I'm not. Aunt Mary needs company every year, left alone in this kitchen to cook for hours and then spend the rest of the night scrubbing pots. I came to help her."

"And get a square meal in the process," said Aunt Mary, Tipper Malone's wife and, some said, the brains behind the success of Malone's Tavern. She gave Sheila a kiss and a pat and then reached for the stewpot. "Can I get you a bowl, Sheila?"

"No, thanks, Aunt Mary. I had supper already. Where's Dad?"

"Dancing, last I saw him," answered Larkin, easing his lanky body back down onto one of the kitchen stools. "But he's been calling for you for hours. You're late."

"I was held up at work."

Larkin caught her hand before she could slip past him. "You'll come back, right? I haven't seen you in weeks, Sis. I was hoping we could talk."

"About your grades?" Sheila asked, laughing. "Do you need help with math again?"

"No. I thought you might have something you'd like to get off your chest this time. I read your name in the paper, then Dad told me what happened. You must be—"

"I'm okay," Sheila said firmly. "I don't need my hand held, Lark."

"An accident like that isn't something you get over easily," her brother argued gently.

"It wasn't an accident," she snapped, pulling her hand free. "It happened because I let it happen! *I* pulled the trigger. I can live with that, dammit. If you can't—well, that's your problem!"

Struck silent by the violence of her response, Larkin looked doubtful, chewing on his lower lip. Aunt Mary's plump face was a mask of sympathy. Sheila wished she could snatch back the moment—at least to soften her tone—but it was too late.

Softly, Larkin told her, "Sheila, we're all on your side, you know. If you decide to—"

"I'm fine," she replied hurriedly, hoping to put an end to their concern. "Really, I'm feeling good." She pushed on the swinging door, saying, "I've got to find Dad. See you later."

Malone's Tavern was like an old-time saloon, with double frosted-glass front doors that opened onto the busy street-corner, beckoning passersby into its warm, homey depths. The main room was paneled in burnished mahogany, beamed with thick slabs of oak and lighted by antique lanterns, and had a high tin-plated ceiling and a magnificent teak bar that curved along the forty feet from the front door to the kitchen. The parquet floor was scuffed by years of traffic—everything from the heavy work boots of steel-workers to the high heels of young secretaries who stopped in for a libation before going home. On one long wall hung black-and-white photos of racehorses—mostly winners of the Irish Derby or the Grand National. A beveled mirror commanded the wall behind the bar, reflecting the faces of the regular patrons—faces that showed the mixture of people who lived in the neighborhood. Italian and Polish, Irish and black, Hispanic and Jew—they all came to Malone's.

Tommy Malone was the center of attention in the bar when Sheila arrived. He had happily draped his long arms over the shoulders of two of the tenors and was lifting his own rather shaky baritone to the tune of "Molly Malone." The rest of the patrons were singing along with him and swinging their beer mugs in time to the music. The noise was deafening.

The light from the kitchen cast Sheila in silhouette for an instant, drawing her father's attention in midlyric. He recognized her at once and promptly changed the words of the song to "Sheila Malone" which set off a roar of laughter among the crowd. Sheila was accustomed to her father's theatrics and accepted the song graciously. When he concluded the last chorus, she threaded her way through the heaving crush and wrapped her arms around his neck and gave her dad a big, crowd-pleasing kiss. Everyone roared and stamped.

"Sheila, my girl," her father shouted in her ear, "you're looking lovely tonight, as usual!"

"I look like hell, but you're too drunk to see it, Dad!" she shouted back, smiling. "How much whiskey have you had?"

"Not as much as you think," he yelled, winking broadly. "But you don't make a profit on a night like this unless you play to the crowd, y'know. Can I get you a beer, my girl?"

"No, Dad, I—"

"Your friend is here," he shouted, raising his voice as the trio struck up "By the Rising of the Moon."

Sheila couldn't hear her father over the music and bent closer, cupping her ear. "What did you say?"

"Your friend!" he bellowed, scanning the crowd that jostled around them. "The nice young man!"

"Who, Dad?"

"Max!"

"*Max?* Max *Bollinger?*"

"Aha!" Tommy cried, waving over the heads of the mob. "There he is! Max! Max, come over here!"

Sheila wanted to melt into the floor—or bolt for the kitchen. But she couldn't have fought her way through that crowd if her life depended on it. In the next second her father was throwing an exuberant arm across Max's broad shoulders and pulling him up to the bar like a prodigal son. Max had a wide, delighted smile on his face and a gleam of excited pleasure in his dark eyes. He looked devilishly handsome in a black leather jacket, a red open-necked shirt and snug jeans that drew the eyes of two women perched on barstools behind him.

"Max, here's my beautiful daughter!" shouted Tommy, pulling Sheila by her arm. "Take care of her now, will you?"

Sheila managed to jam her hands against Max's chest before the crowd crushed them together. Their bodies collided, and a second later Max was laughing and slipping his hard knee between Sheila's thighs.

"Sheila love, I've missed you," he said, wrapping his arms around her and drawing her close for a sizzling kiss.

She fought him, of course, but couldn't do any real damage—not with her father watching like some kind of victorious matchmaker and half the patrons of the bar applauding. In the end she gave up, letting Max part her mouth, holding her head still with his hands thrust into the tumble of her hair. It was a tremendous kiss—fiery and sweet at the same time, with Max's lean frame pressed intimately against Sheila's softer body. It made her heart pound, her senses swim.

Push him away, she told herself. But couldn't.

At last he set her down, his mocking, amused gaze locked on hers as if they were alone, not surrounded by bedlam. Sheila clung to him instinctively, and Tommy pounded Max on the back as if he'd hit a home run.

Max loved the expression on her face—half angry, half dazed with passion. Her full mouth looked blurred from his kiss.

"I *have* missed you," Max repeated, ignoring her father and barely audible over the noise of the party. "Where's the outfit you bought? Not that this doesn't make my mouth water, but—"

"You have a lot of guts coming here," she retorted, glaring up at him. "When you know you're not wanted!"

"Not wanted?" he shouted back, laughing. "I've been made to feel like a member of the family!"

"Half the *city* feels like a member of this family tonight. I told you not to come!"

"Your voice said no, but your eyes said yes." He filled his hands with her hair and caressed her. "Sheila, you feel wonderful. What do you say we blow this pop stand?"

She must have realized she was still gripping his jacket, because she let go abruptly. She couldn't pull out of his embrace, however, for the crowd still forced them together. "You shouldn't be here," she shouted. "I don't want to see you anymore."

He laughed. "Why stop now? We've hit it off so well—"

"Shut up, will you? I mean it, this time, Max! I can't hang around with you."

Still grinning, he persisted, "Darling, we don't have a choice. It's fate, don't you see? Kismet. You surprised me in the shower, and ever since then I've—"

"You aren't listening!" Sheila shouted, pushing out of his grasp. "Get out of my life!"

Max finally realized something was wrong and tightened his grip on her arms. "What's the matter?"

"You, blast it! You're a criminal, and I'm a cop! That means we're on opposite sides!"

"What the hell are you talking about?"

"I know all about you, Max—"

"What?"

"So just leave me alone. Nothing good can happen between us."

"Will you make some sense, please. I— Oh, hell, I can't hear a thing in here. Let's go."

He seized Sheila's elbow and steered her into the crowd. She fought him, but rather than punch one of her father's patrons, she soon gave up and let Max push her to the door. On the sidewalk, she spun around to face him.

"Damn you, Max, I've learned all about Enrique Furmire." Continuing, despite the people passing by on the sidewalk, Sheila said, "If stealing jewelry from your own mother isn't enough—"

"You can't prove that I stole jewelry from anyone, for God's sake!"

"What about Enrique Furmire?"

For Max, hearing the man's name was like getting punched in the gut. "That scum? What about him?"

"He's dead, that's what!" Sheila's face was taut, her eyes sparkling with anger. "He's been dead for four years, and imagine my surprise when I hear he probably died a few days before you left town for Germany!"

"What's that supposed to mean?"

"It means you're suspected of killing him, of course!"

"*Killing* him? Do you believe that?"

"I'm a cop," she snapped. "I believe facts."

Max thought fast. How much did she know? Had she managed to get ahead of him already? And was she working alone? Or did half the police force know about his connection to Enrique Furmire?

He forced himself to sound composed. "Just what are the facts in this case? What proof has anyone got that I even *knew* Enrique Furmire?"

"Did you?"

Better give her something—but not enough to hang him. "I knew who he was, yes. He used to hassle my father on a regular basis."

"For money your father borrowed, right?"

"Right. But—"

"And you were in terrible financial shape at the time, so what's stopping ambitious young Max from bashing the head of the loan shark on some dark, convenient night so that your precious family business can—"

"You haven't got a shred of evidence against me," Max exploded, suddenly confident that she was fishing for information he was damned if he'd give. "Furmire was a lowlife—a common criminal who was mixed up in Lord knows that kind of crime. No doubt one of his charming associates killed him."

He grabbed Sheila hard, and bending close to her angry face, he swore to her, "I didn't kill anybody, Sheila."

"Until I can prove that, I want you out of my life."

"I wish I could accommodate you," he said simply.

Sheila blew up. "Why are you acting this way? We don't even *know* each other!"

"We know enough," declared Max, cutting her off. "I can't stop thinking about you, and I know it's the same for you. We both like mystery, Sheila. That's why we're drawn together. I don't know—it's exciting, it's magnetic. I *like* not knowing everything about you yet."

His words sparked a realization in Sheila. He was right, perhaps—not knowing him made Max more appealing somehow. She couldn't explain it. The thought scared her a little, but she brought herself up short, striving to plaster her cop persona into place before the situation turned even more volatile. "I have to know your involvement in the two crimes, Max."

"Why?"

"Because I do! It's my job!"

"It's also your obsession, right?"

"I—'

"Can you think about anything but me?" he asked, coming closer and catching her arm again. "When you're at work, when you're walking home, when you're in bed at night, you're thinking about Max, aren't you?"

"It's my job!"

"The hell it is. Not in this situation. You're not assigned to either one of those cases, are you?"

"I can still think about them—and you."

"That's just your excuse."

"It also happens to be the truth."

"Want to hear another truth?" He pulled her close, aligning their bodies. "It's the same with me, Sheila. I'm

trying to get my business going again, fix up my apartment, get my things out of storage, but all I can see in my
mind is you! I see your face, your sad smile and your scared
eyes, and I want to be with you!"

"Stop it."

"I can't. I'm drawn to you. It's not just sex, either.
There's something about you that fits a need in me. You
feel it, too, don't you?"

"I don't understand."

"Neither do I, but I like it. Maybe you're drawn to me
because I'm a puzzle—something you can solve. But until
the pieces are in place, you can't get me out of your head,
can you?"

Sheila squeezed her eyes shut tight. "No, I can't."

Max's hands held her firmly. "It's exciting, isn't it?"

"It scares me!"

"Because you're out of control, that's all. We both are.
But we won't get hurt, Sheila. We might as well relax and
enjoy it."

"*Enjoy* it? Enjoy being miserable? Unable to think or
work or study? What's to enjoy?"

"This, for one thing," replied Max, and he kissed her
again.

Sheila could have kicked her way free. She could have
struggled against him and ended the contact at once. But
she didn't. She let the kiss happen, let it sweep over her like
a huge, washing wave of sensual delight. Max's body felt
hard and good against hers. His hands kneaded her shoulders and smoothed down her back. His mouth tasted delicious and hot, his tongue teasing; his lips rough, yet
coaxing.

Sheila responded instinctively—arching her body into
his, wrapping her arms around his neck and kissing him
back with all the fire that blazed inside her.

When the kiss burned itself out, they leaned unsteadily against each other, breathing in gasps.

Max cursed under his breath. "Let's go someplace."

"I can't."

"I want you, Sheila. Damn the consequences. I want to make love with you."

"Maybe I want you, too," she responded unevenly. "But I won't let it happen. Not now."

"When?"

She lifted her gaze to his and knew by Max's taut expression, how urgently he wanted to take her to bed. "When the puzzle is solved," she said at last. "Until then, we can't be together."

"Sheila—"

"I'm a cop, Max, and the daughter of a cop. I've got a code to live by, and going to bed or anywhere else with you would violate that code."

"But you want me—we want each other! Lord, I can feel how your heart is beating—"

"I can fight that. I can fight you, if I have to. Don't force me, Max."

He released her slowly, finally seeing the resolve in her face. "All right, I won't. But I'm not going to make this easy on you, Sheila." Kissing her mouth fleetingly, he said, "I may be committing suicide by wanting you this way, but I intend to have you."

Six

On Friday, Cowboy said the words that made Sheila's heart freeze.

"Hey, partner, Lieutenant Fiske said the Furmire murder is ours."

Sheila folded her hands on her desk and attempted to look only mildly surprised. "Since when are we calling it a murder? I thought Furmire only disappeared."

Cowboy plunked himself on the edge of her desk. "That's the official story, but the lieutenant is willing to listen to us if we come up with anything that proves otherwise."

"Why us?"

Cowboy laughed. "Why not us? We know Bollinger. We're as close to the murder as any other cop still working this precinct. Besides, I gave Fiske the impression that I had some spare time and wanted this case bad. Why do you ask? You got something against this Furmire business?"

"No," Sheila answered hastily, hoping Cowboy would not guess that her relationship with Max Bollinger had definitely grown beyond the bounds of cop and suspect. She asked, "What's your first move?"

Cowboy reached for his coat. "Let's go talk to Maxie."

"What? Now?"

"Sure. What's the matter? You have a little too much green beer last night?"

Sheila grabbed her jacket and followed Cowboy down the stairs. She had a splitting headache, but she wasn't going to mention it to Cowboy. Her condition was not caused by drinking anything, but rather the turmoil that had been swimming around in her mind since the last time she'd been with Max.

Something he had said was bugging the hell out of her. *You're drawn to me because I'm a puzzle.*

He was only half right. The puzzle appealed to her, but Sheila also knew that she'd never been so physically attracted to a man in her life. Still, the fact that he challenged her mentally was what made him impossible to thrust out of her mind.

He was a puzzle, all right—a damn sexy puzzle.

She kept quiet during the ride to the Bollinger brewery. Cowboy cranked up the volume of the radio until a jungle-beat rock-and-roll song filled the car. He didn't comment on Sheila's silence. After years of partnering together, they were comfortable not filling every minute with chatter. They checked Max's place of residence first. Sheila played dumb while Cowboy located the door and pounded on it a few times. When nobody came to answer, they headed across the alley into the old brewery, where a few lights could be seen.

The brewery's entrance was large enough to drive a truck through. Someone had left the big doors hanging open, so the building was very cold. Sheila shoved her hands into the pockets of her jacket and followed Cowboy inside, telling herself that the only reason she was shivering was the lack of heat. Half a dozen huge crates had been unloaded just inside. Sheila noted they bore labels in both English and German.

"Hello!" Cowboy called as they strolled past the crates. His voice echoed eerily in the cavernous building. "Anybody home?"

"The place is empty," Sheila concluded. "Why don't we find someplace else to start this investigation?"

"What's the matter with you, Malone? Afraid you're going to catch Maxie in his altogether again?"

"Afraid?" Sheila mustered some sarcasm. "Did you get a look at the guy, Cowboy?"

Her partner sniffed. "He wasn't my type. Hey! Anybody here?"

No one answered, but from down the corridor, Sheila and Cowboy simultaneously heard voices raised. Cowboy looked at her, his eyebrows rising. "Sounds like somebody's having a little tiff, doesn't it?"

Sheila listened, recognizing Max's voice as the low rumble that responded to the higher-pitched voice that was raised in petulant pleading.

Cowboy jerked his head in the direction of the argument, and they tiptoed down the concrete corridor to a row of offices. They were all open and empty, with a few pieces of old furniture left in a few of them. In the last office, a light was burning.

"Dammit, Cameron," Sheila heard Max's voice saying, "you're going to have to cut the apron strings sooner or later."

"That's what I'm telling you, Max! All I want is a few bucks and a place to crash for a while—"

"You're welcome to stay with me," Max cut in firmly, "but I certainly can't float you for—"

"I can't live with you! I was hoping to get my own apartment. I found this great place downtown. It's got skylights and a pool—"

Max laughed. "Cameron, I can buy you an occasional dinner, but I can't afford rent for myself, let alone you right now. Won't Mother give you—"

"She won't give me anything. We've had another fight. I—"

The younger man's voice was silenced, as if Max had suddenly signaled him to be quiet. Sheila figured their presence was known, so she goosed Cowboy, who stepped through the office doorway with a pleasant smile. The room was sparsely furnished with an old desk, a couple of leather chairs and two file cabinets. A vintage telephone sat on the desk and was surrounded by papers—an indication that Max had been interrupted at work.

A young man lolled in one of the chairs, while standing behind the desk was none other than Max himself. Sheila braced herself, wondering what the first words out of Max's mouth would be.

"Hello," he greeted mildly, his gaze traveling from Cowboy to Sheila and back again. "It's Detectives Stankowsky and Malone, right?"

Sheila released an inaudible sigh of relief.

"Right," said Cowboy, grinning broadly in an imitation of the not-too-bright cop stumbling onto something fishy. "How're you doing, Bollinger? Nice to see you again—and better dressed this time, too. Who's this?"

The slender young man lounged to his feet. He was very good-looking in a blond beach-boy kind of way. He wore an expensive Italian suit with polished loafers, and an earring in one ear. His hair was gathered into a ponytail and his face was narrow and classically handsome, with an aristocratic nose, a mobile mouth, photogenic cheekbones and dark eyes. Dark, Bollinger eyes, Sheila thought at once.

"This is my brother Cameron," said Max. "Cameron Pletheridge."

"Pletheridge?" Cowboy repeated, putting out his hand for the younger man to shake. "That must make you half brothers, right? What's the age difference between you two guys?"

"Ten years," replied Max. "My parents were divorced when I was quite young. Cameron and our sister Cathy are my mother's second family."

"There's hardly anyone from the old married-with-two-kids school, huh? Nice to meet you, Cam. I'm Detective Stankowsky. This is my partner, Detective Malone."

Again Sheila held her breath, wondering what Max might have told his brother about her. But Cameron appeared not to recognize her name and simply put on a womanizer's smile and shook her hand slowly.

"Hi," he said, in a lighter version of Max's baritone. Oozing sex appeal, he added, "I've never met a police-woman before. And I never expected one to be so beautiful."

"We come in all shapes and sizes."

"I like your shape a lot," he remarked, and smiled some more. "You must work out every day."

Sheila extricated her hand from Cameron's. "Not really. Do you live with your mother, Cameron?"

Her question caused a look of surprise to appear on Cameron's pretty-boy face. "Me? Why, uh, yeah, I guess you could say I do now and then."

"Do you have an apartment elsewhere, too?"

"No, just a room at her place at the moment. But it's only temporary. A couple of weeks that's all."

Max was finally starting to smile. "What's all this about, Detectives? Has there been some progress in solving the theft of my mother's jewelry?"

"Not that we know of," Cowboy answered pleasantly.

Max looked toughly handsome next to his elegant brother. He was dressed in a plain blue work shirt with a maroon knit tie knotted loosely at the neck. His khaki trousers looked suitable for rough work. He stood in a relaxed stance with his hands braced on his hips. "Then what can I do for you?" he asked. "Or have you come looking for Cameron today?"

"We came to see you," Cowboy answered, "but maybe Cam would like to stick around—"

"I'm sure he's got things to do elsewhere. Right, Cameron?"

"Uh, sure."

Max inclined his head, a gesture that told his brother to hit the road. As the younger man picked up his expensive overcoat in preparation to leave, Max turned to Sheila and Cowboy. "What's this all about then? Shall I make us a pot of coffee before we get started?"

Max was making an effort to sound hospitable, but actually he wanted to order the detectives to get the hell out of his office. How much had they overheard? How much had he actually said to Cameron? He couldn't guess anything by Sheila's expression. She was busy with her Sergeant Friday imitation, complete with stone face and disquietingly penetrating eyes.

"This won't take long enough for coffee," Cowboy replied. "We're wondering if you can tell us where you were the week of November twenty-third, four years ago."

Cameron looked hastily at Max, then ducked for the door and escaped without saying goodbye. When he was gone, Max said, "I can't remember."

"You can't? It was the week of Thanksgiving," Cowboy prompted. "Sometimes people remember what they did on holidays. Since this was just the day before—"

"My family doesn't really celebrate Thanksgiving," Max said smoothly. "It's been a decade since we had turkey and all the trimmings. It was a week like any other, I assume."

"Do you keep a calendar?" Cowboy pressed. "A way of keeping track of business appointments, maybe?"

"Of course. Now that you mention it, I may still have one for that year. I keep them for tax purposes."

"Is it handy?"

Max smiled slightly. *How much did they know already?* It was probably best to tell the truth whenever possible, he decided. That way he could remember what he'd said when it came time to start lying.

"I'm not exactly sure where it is," he answered. "I had all my belongings packed and stored while I was in Germany. I'm just now starting to go through those things. I might be able to put my hands on it in a few days."

"Would you do that?"

Max looked at Cowboy for a while. "How about telling me what this is all about, Detective?"

Sheila said, "Do you recognize the name Enrique Furmire?"

Max tried to read what she was doing. Why play dumb? She had something to hide now, too, he supposed, and damned himself for getting her involved.

Still managing a measured voice, he responded, "Enrique Furmire was a criminal. My father, unfortunately, was mixed up with the man."

"How?"

"My father's financial troubles are a matter of public record. He was close to bankruptcy for years and borrowed money wherever he could get it. Furmire loaned cash, but at exorbitant interest rates. He also encouraged my father to begin gambling with what little capital our company had left."

Max tried to control the undercurrent of bitterness he heard in his own words. He continued, "My father's finances quickly fell apart after he began dealing with Furmire. In December, my father died."

"Are you aware that Furmire died also?" Cowboy asked.

"I know he disappeared," Max replied.

"We believe he was killed," Cowboy went on. "By someone who had a reason for wanting him dead."

"Are you asking me if I killed him?"

"Did you?"

Max smiled coldly, knowing at last that they'd come on a fishing expedition, nothing more. "No, I didn't kill him."

"Do you have any information that might help us find out who killed him?"

For a split second, Max wondered if he might learn more if he joined forces with the police. But he quickly discarded the thought. They might lock him up for a while, and that he could not tolerate.

He said, "No."

Back at the precinct, Sheila wasn't thinking straight. She used up nearly half a bottle of correction fluid while typing up a burglary report. And when her telephone rang, she nearly knocked it on the floor as she made a grab for the receiver.

"Detective Malone."

In her ear, Max's voice said, "I think we'd better talk."

Even the man's voice seemed to turn her nerves into jelly!
She couldn't speak for an instant, then managed to croak,
"About what?"

"That little farce we played this afternoon, for one thing.
When do you get off work?"

"Half an hour ago." Cowboy sat at his desk less than ten
feet away, so she cupped the receiver close and told him, "I
can be finished here in fifteen minutes."

"Then meet me at your father's place."

She didn't get a chance to argue. Max hung up.

If she'd had the time to explain, she'd have told Max that
the last place she wanted to be seen with him was at Malone's Tavern. But since she had no choice, she stood on the
sidewalk in front of the bar and hoped that neither her father nor Uncle Tipper could see her through the windows.

Max came ten minutes later, and when he came strolling
up, Sheila guessed that he had intentionally forced her to
advertise her presence outside the tavern. He had a das-
tardly gleam in his eye. He also looked devastatingly
handsome in his leather jacket with a black sweater underneath it.

He caught her arm and deposited a hard kiss on Sheila's
mouth. "Looking for a desperate criminal?"

Sheila's lips tingled, and the rest of her body didn't feel
too steady, either. "I think I've found him. I'm not going
to waste time with you, Max. I want—"

He laughed shortly. "You think you're in a position to
demand anything from me? I played along with you today. What was that all about, anyway? Are you afraid your
partner will think we're having an affair?"

"Max, I'm serious. I'm not in the habit of— Where are
we going?"

He had pulled her to the door and was leading her into
Malone's Tavern. "To get some dinner. And you're pay-

ing, by the way. You owe me that much, and I'm broke anyway."

She grabbed his sleeve. "Not in here, Max! Please, anywhere but here."

He stopped, looking at Sheila with a calculating grin. "Anywhere?"

Hurriedly, she explained, "I don't want my father to see us together."

"Are you ashamed of me, Sheila?"

"I feel very uncomfortable seeing you at all, and you know it. It's unethical. My dad was a cop. He won't understand what I'm doing."

"Do you?"

Sheila forced herself to look at Max. "No, I don't. But we're beyond that now, aren't we?"

"I think so. I'm surprised to hear you say it, though."

"No more surprised than I am. Let's get out of here, all right? For whatever reasons, I don't want to get caught."

Max tucked her hand into the crook of his elbow and they set off walking briskly up the street. "All right, we'll keep ourselves a secret a little while longer. I'm starved, are you?"

Grimly, she replied, "I haven't been able to eat since I met you."

He laughed and pulled her along the sidewalk. "Then we'll have to tempt your appetite, won't we?"

"Max," she began.

They walked a few paces together, then he answered, "Yes?"

Sheila steeled herself to speak. "I'm sorry about today. I should have told Cowboy about seeing you before and how we—we've gotten to know each other better. But I haven't been able to do that yet."

"Because you think I'm a murderer?"

"I don't think you're a murderer," she said, before she could consider the words.

"Do you mean that?"

No, Sheila didn't know what she meant, but poking into her own psyche hadn't been working well lately. "I— I don't know for sure. My instincts say you're not, but I can't tell my partner that, can I? He'll say I'm thinking with some other organ besides my brain. He'll think you're trying to seduce me so I'll take your side against the rest of the police department."

"Do you think he's right?"

"Are you asking if I think you're manipulating me."

"Am I?"

"I can't— Oh, dammit, why am I defending you? *You* tell *me* why I should trust you!"

"Maybe you shouldn't. Maybe we should stop everything right now, say goodbye and—"

"This is a switch!" She laughed and stopped on the sidewalk. "What's going on?"

"I want you to understand what you're doing," Max replied, facing her under the traffic light. "I want you going into this relationship with your eyes wide open."

"Relationship? Is that what we're doing?"

"It's what I'm doing," said Max firmly. "So—do you trust me or don't you?"

"I shouldn't," Sheila answered. She stepped off the curb and started walking again, her head down.

Max wondered if he should be feeling like a rat. He didn't. Being with Sheila seemed to drown out the voice of his conscience. He hustled to catch up with her.

"You have to admit there's a sexual attraction between us. It's got to be based on something besides a simple chemical reaction. Maybe it's trust."

"That would be a laugh, wouldn't it?"

"Something's bringing us together, Sheila. I think we need each other."

"I don't need anybody."

"I felt the same way until I met you. I'm a loner, I admit. I like beautiful women and good conversation and great sex and all of that. But I've never felt driven to make one woman my own—until I met you. You're strong and sassy and smart and— Oh, I can't explain it. I want you."

"Max—"

"You need me, too, I think."

Sheila faltered to a stop again, and closed her eyes. "Damn you," she muttered.

Max stopped in front of her, and took hold of her arms. "Nobody else can make you feel better about what happened that night in the park. But with me, you feel good enough to stop thinking about it all the time, right?"

Sheila didn't answer for a while. He thought he saw a gleam of tears in her eyes for a second, but she must have willed them to evaporate.

At last she took a breath and admitted, "When I'm with you, I find myself feeling that maybe I have a life away from the job. Maybe I can put shooting a man behind me."

Max's heart turned over in his chest. In that moment he decided to tell her everything. Maybe she could help, maybe she couldn't. But he knew he couldn't keep any more secrets from her.

He said, "I think we just found a place to start."

He took her arm again and guided Sheila down the side street, then turned into the alley. At last, he took a set of keys from his pocket and shoved one into a door.

"This is your place," Sheila observed, beside him.

"Can't fool a detective, can I?"

"I thought you wanted dinner."

"I thought you said we could go anywhere but your father's."

She hung back. "I didn't mean this, Max."

Smiling down at her, he pushed the door wide. "*I* did."

"But we can talk in a public place."

"A public place like a restaurant where your partner might stroll in? A bar where your superior officer hangs out?"

Sheila bit her lip. "If I'm going to break rules, I guess I don't want to alert the entire police force. We're just going to talk, right?" She stated firmly, "I don't know you well enough for anything else."

"We'll change that." Max maneuvered her inside and closed the door. He took her hand. "This way."

Sheila let him lead the way, praying she could resist any advances he might make. Her one consolation was knowing that Max's apartment wasn't suited to seduction. When she'd last seen the place, it had been as bare as a fire hall—the lair of a lone wolf. But one step inside, and Sheila was gulping with concern. He had dragged out the furniture and created a comfortable living space out of all that emptiness. The workmen had finished hanging kitchen cabinets in one corner, and he'd pushed a big trestle table nearby. In the middle of the floor on a thick green rug were arranged a couple of comfortable easy chairs, a lamp, a low table and a stack of books and papers that indicated where Max had spent the past few evenings.

He'd also gotten himself a bed.

Set diagonally in a secluded alcove at the far end of the loft was a huge unmade bed tumbled with striped sheets and a pile of quilts. Judging by the number of bedclothes, the loft got very cold at night.

Max saw Sheila's moment of hesitation. Without asking, he peeled her jacket off and dropped it with his own over the railing. "Welcome to my humble train station."

"It still looks huge," Sheila remarked, rubbing her hands together as if to warm them. "But you've made some improvements."

"I won't take the credit," he replied, already heading for the kitchen. "My sister was here yesterday and arranged everything. Without her, I'd still be using a sleeping bag."

Sheila followed him. "I was surprised to hear you mention a sister today. I've been under the impression that you're one of a kind."

"Oh, I am. You'll see. Cathy's my half sister, actually. She and Cameron—"

"Are the children of your mother's second husband."

"Right. Cathy's the best thing that resulted from that marriage. She's twenty-two and a darling." Max dug into the refrigerator and came up with two bottles of beer. He displayed the Steel City Ale label to her. When she nodded her approval, Max opened both of them. "Sorry, no glasses yet," he said. "Do you mind?"

"Me?" Sheila accepted one of the frosty bottles from him. "I'm the one from the wrong side of the tracks, remember? I haven't got your champagne tastes."

Max clinked his bottle against hers. "Are you implying that I've got expensive tastes?"

"Sure. You go to the opera on Saturday nights, drive that luxurious car, and then there's the—"

He laughed at the idea. "I'm the son of a brewer!"

"The rich son of a *rich* brewer. You're an American aristocrat, Mr. Bollinger."

He took a long swallow of beer, amused that she'd think of him that way. "What do you know about aristocrats?"

"Let's not talk about me. I don't want to show how ignorant I am of things that you take for granted." She sipped her beer. "This is good stuff. And as the daughter of a bartender, I know what I'm talking about when it comes to beer."

Max turned away and set about lighting a fire that had already been laid in the kitchen hearth. He used a match to ignite a wad of newspaper that had been stuffed under the logs and kindling. In a moment, a cheery flame sprang up.

Watching Max dust off his hands, she drank a little more beer and said, "Tell me more about your sister and brother."

"What do you want to know?"

"Cameron seemed like a nice kid."

Max laughed easily and led the way to the upholstered chairs. "Cameron is anything but a nice kid. He's twenty-five going on thirteen, in lots of ways."

"Spoiled?"

"You picked that up? Yes, he's spoiled. I've contributed to that, I guess. It's easier to bail him out of trouble than to make sure he doesn't get into it in the first place. He and my mother are a pair."

Sheila slid into one of the easy chairs, curling her long legs under her body to get comfortable. "What's your mother like?"

Max sat down opposite her, pushing a pile of papers onto the rug to make room for himself. "Mother's a character. You saw how she behaves—half Joan Crawford and half lost-waif. Everything's theater for her."

"I thought her faint was a little overdone."

"She has always milked her delicate constitution for all it was worth. To make up for her physical weaknesses, she's got a brain like a barracuda's. That's why she divorced my father in the first place."

"What d'you mean?"

"She hated being broke. She met Pletheridge at a country club function and married him four months later. My father never knew what hit him." It was true. Max couldn't help thinking that his mother's remarriage must have contributed to his father's decline. But that was water under the bridge. He couldn't hold his mother's behavior against her. "Ironically, Pletheridge hasn't been doing very well lately, I hear."

"His business is in trouble?"

Max shrugged. "That's what Cameron tells me. My little brother's panicked he won't get his inheritance, I guess."

"What's Cathy like?"

Max smiled and sat forward, bracing his elbows on his knees. "Cathy's a gem. She graduated from the university last year and got a job as a commercial artist downtown."

"I thought I detected an artist's touch here."

Max glanced around at the loft—at the crackling fire and the work his sister had done arranging his belongings. "She's got a good eye, I think. Not to mention a sensitive soul. While I was living in Germany, she wrote me a letter every week. Nobody else did that. She's grown up a lot since I've been away, but if it's possible, she's turned out even nicer than before."

"You must love her a lot."

Surprised, Max asked, "Didn't I say that?"

"Essentially, yes, I guess," Sheila admitted, smiling.

Max saw her smile, but couldn't help noticing the trace of melancholy that lingered in Sheila's lovely green eyes. He said to her, "I'm glad she graduated from the university last year. If she hadn't, she could have been one of the students your rapist attacked."

Sheila's smile faded, and she looked away. She shook her head wearily. "Let's not talk about that."

"We don't have to," Max agreed gently, watching her face. "I've been thinking about it, though. You see, Cathy's the one person I couldn't stand to see hurt. If she'd been one of the victims of that lowlife—"

"But she wasn't."

"She could have been," Max insisted. "It's pure luck, isn't it? How does a man like that choose a victim?"

"Randomly, I'm sure."

"So Cathy could have been the one he grabbed. I love her a lot, Sheila. I'm glad somebody protected her from that guy. I'm glad you did what you had to do."

She let out a short, unamused laugh. "That's not something I hear every day."

"Maybe you need to hear it more often. Thank you, Sheila. I'm glad you did your job. You saved me from doing it."

"What's that supposed to mean?"

"It means I'd go after him myself if he hurt my sister. I love her and I want to be sure she's protected. I'd have to see that he was punished for what he did to her."

"I didn't act out of revenge," Sheila said sharply. "It's not my job to punish anyone. That's for a judge or jury to decide. I was supposed to bring him to justice."

"You didn't get the chance. You had to protect yourself in a life-or-death situation, so you reacted the way you'd been trained to react."

Sheila rubbed her eyes with the palm of her hand. "I know all this," she said, half talking to herself as well as Max. "I know I did what I had to do, and I can live with it. That's not the problem."

"What *is* the problem?"

Sheila hesitated.

After a moment of silence broken only by the quiet snapping of the nearby fire, Max remarked, "It must be tough being a cop and a woman at the same time."

She looked at him cautiously. "Why do you say that?"

"Do you disagree?"

"No, I just— I'm comfortable with my job. I can do the work, and I do it pretty well. But sometimes it's easier just pretending to be a man."

The idea startled Max. "Is that what you do?"

She shrugged. "Sometimes. A lot of the time, to be honest. Being a cop isn't a job that makes you feel terribly feminine."

"That getup you were wearing Saturday night could hardly be called manly."

"The hooker outfit? That's different. I'm playing a role when I'm dressed like that. The rest of the time, I wear jeans and boots and talk like a sailor."

Softly, Max questioned, "Why do you suppose you're trying so hard not to be a woman?"

"I *like* being female," Sheila responded. "It's not that. Up until now, I was happy with everything that goes with being a woman. But now, I— Lord, I can't put on a skirt anymore. I never wear makeup unless I'm supposed to put some on. I keep my hair pulled back or hidden under a hat. I was thinking of getting it cut—"

"Don't do that," Max said quickly. "It's beautiful, Sheila."

"I don't want to be beautiful," she blurted out. "It's too—too—"

"What?"

"Scary," she admitted at last. "When I'm looking feminine, I'm scared. It's dumb, but it's true."

Max shook his head. "It's not dumb. It's understandable. You've seen a lot of bad things happen to women lately."

She stared at the beer swirling in the bottle she held. "I never expected so many of the victims to be female. Almost all of the calls I get involve women getting beaten up or cut or raped or— Lord, sometimes we take bets on how many calls we'll get before we finally hit one that's a male victim!"

Puzzled, Max asked, "Men don't get hurt?"

"Men get murdered," Sheila said. "Four times out of five, a murder victim in this town will be male. But women get everything else. And because I'm a woman, I get sent out as a decoy a lot of the time. Tomorrow, I'm supposed to stand on a street corner waiting for a psycho to come after me with a knife, and while I'm standing there I'll be hoping like hell that my partner can tackle him first, but not *too* soon."

"What do you mean?"

"If I whip out my badge or gun too soon, we blow it. I have to give the creep what he wants so we catch him in the act and get a conviction."

"That must go against every instinct you have."

"But I've got to hang tough. We work for weeks setting up a case, and if I chicken out at the last minute, all those man-hours are down the drain."

Max considered her explanation thoughtfully. "So when you're a woman, you're a victim. And when you're pretending to be a man, you're okay, is that it?"

"In a way, that's it."

"Are you having any trouble doing that?" Max indicated her clothes. "I mean, here you are wearing jeans and your father's castoffs, with your hair pulled back and—"

Sheila grinned wryly. "You sure know how to compliment a woman, don't you?"

Her smile sent a warm, liquid sensation curling up Max's spine. "You know what I mean. You're suppressing a lot of femininity under that hard-nosed cop routine, Sheila. It must wear you out. Is that why you went shopping for something pretty the other day? For relief?"

"I don't know what the hell I was doing. Then *you* came along and— Oh, damn, it didn't matter what I was wearing anymore."

"You looked wonderful, Sheila. It was a side of you that took my breath away."

"I didn't come here for sweet talk."

"But sweet talk is part of being a woman, right? Are you afraid to be a woman with me, Sheila?"

Hell, yes, she wanted to say. But not for the same reasons she shunned all feminine things when she was working. With Max, she felt sexy. And the sexy feeling made her reckless. Unsteadily she set down her beer bottle. Just the sound of gentleness in his voice was having a disastrous effect on her self-control.

Softly, Max told her, "You can't deny it forever, Sheila."

"What can't I deny?"

"That you're a woman who's capable of everything a woman should be. Sexual desire, for one thing."

"Max—"

"I can't help it," he said, staying in his chair but looking more and more like he wanted to spring out of it. "When I'm with you, I invariably start thinking about sex. You're doing it, too."

A little breathlessly, Sheila laughed again. "Who do you think you are—a mind reader?"

"I can see it in your pretty green eyes, Sheila. You're attracted to me."

Good guess, she almost said.

"And we both know I'm attracted to you," Max continued. "Despite your efforts to hide it, you're beautiful and sexy and strong. Strangely enough, you're vulnerable, too. That's the part that makes you irresistible. I want you more than I've wanted a woman in years."

Maybe he wanted to appear smooth and sophisticated, but Sheila heard the sandpapery hoarseness that entered his voice. She could see that he wasn't cool on the inside.

"Fortunately, we're both adults," she pointed out, "which means we can control our impulses."

"Speak for yourself," he retorted.

"Max," she started bravely. "You're wonderful for my self-esteem, and I appreciate you trying to help me with my silly psychological problems, but I— I'm not interested in going to bed with you."

"Liar."

She gripped the arms of the chair as if to keep herself from running away—or into his arms. "Okay, maybe I'm lying, but I'm also trying like hell to be sensible."

"Then you *are* attracted to me? Even when I'm not stark naked in the shower?"

She grinned a little. "I have to admit, you look pretty good without your clothes, Mr. Bollinger."

As if she had issued a challenge, Max set down his beer bottle and began to pull his black sweater over his head.

"Wait!" Sheila laughed. "That wasn't a hint! Max, what are you doing?"

"Taking my clothes off," he said, proceeding to yank his tie loose and unbutton his shirt. "If this is what it takes, I'll strip down to nothing right here."

"What do you think you're going to accomplish by this?"

"I want to drive you to distraction," he replied cheerfully, peeling off his shirt. "I'm considered downright irresistible by some women, you know."

He was irresistible, all right. Sheila gulped and squirmed in her chair. "We need some music," she suggested, trying to keep her cool as she watched him toss the shirt onto the floor and stand up. His chest looked magnificent, with the firelight playing over his muscles. Her voice cracking, she said, "Max, you don't have to do this."

He unfastened his belt and tugged it loose from the loops. "Yes, I do."

"I think I'm already as turned on as I can get."

He dropped the belt, came to her and bending down, braced his hands on the overstuffed arms of the chair. "*Are* you?"

As Max scanned her face, his gaze was so penetrating that she was sure he could see all the things she wanted to keep hidden. The flame in his dark eyes made her tremble with suppressed desire. Her hands itched to caress his bare chest, to feel the heat of his skin and the texture of his hair.

"You're driving me wild," she told him.

"That was my intention, sexy lady. I want to kiss you."

"I don't think I could stop you."

"For some reason," Max said, "I want you to make the first move. You're not going to be a victim here, Sheila. Kiss me. Touch me."

Involuntarily she lifted her hands to his chest. His flesh felt warm to her touch, and Sheila's fingertips shook as they skimmed into the crisp hair there. Her heart was pounding, but suddenly she could feel Max's pulse, too. It was racing out of control—a discovery that made Sheila brave.

She wound her arms around his neck and pulled him down into a kiss. His mouth brushed tantalizingly across hers, but he drew back before she could press for more. It was a quick kiss that tested the waters. Sheila looked up into his eyes and felt her breath catch in her throat.

"Lord, you make me feel strange," Max muttered, driving his fingers through her hair and tilting her face up to his. "I want to protect you at the same time I want to drag you into my bed."

"You won't have to drag me."

His hand brushed her hair aside, and Sheila knew he was looking at the vestiges of the bruise left by the man who'd attacked her in the park. His expression was unreadable, then he lowered his mouth to kiss her there—tenderly avoiding any touch that might hurt her, but kissing her with such gentle attention that Sheila began to tremble.

At last, Max pulled Sheila to her feet and wrapped his arms around her in a swift hug. "I want you badly, Sheila. Maybe too badly to be gentle."

"I'm not going to break." She smoothed her palms down the luscious curve of his back in a caress that caused Max to arch erotically against her body. Her insides responded with a sharp, aching stab of desire. On a breath she whispered, "Make love to me, Max."

He cradled Sheila's cheek in one hand to look into her eyes again. "Are we going to regret this?"

She had made her choice when she agreed to come upstairs with him, so she smiled, saying, "I've regretted worse things than this. Let me be reckless tonight."

He eased closer until their mouths hovered centimeters from each other's. His gaze glowed as he read the passion Sheila knew must be obvious in her eyes. "We'll both be reckless."

"Kiss me," Sheila said.

He did, tasting her lips so gently that it was Sheila who parted her mouth and found his tongue with her own. Max made a little noise and pulled her closer so that she wound her arms around his neck to prolong their kiss. She could feel her breasts find a niche against his chest, and her flesh shivered under the caress of his hands on her back. With her own hands, she traced the shape of his muscles, the hardness of his tall body.

In a single, fluid motion, Max lifted Sheila off her feet and carried her across the bare floor to his bed. The familiarity with which he handled her body made Sheila gasp. Setting her down again, he whispered, "Last chance. Do you want us to stop?"

"I've wanted this for a long time, Max."

His dark eyes glinted. "Since you caught me in the shower?"

She stroked his face, wishing she could memorize the expression that she saw there—the desire, the humor, everything that made Max unique. "That wasn't what attracted me to you."

"Then what?"

"Something that happened afterward. With Elke."

"With *Elke*?" Max was laughing, half in the act of unfastening Sheila's sweater. "What's Elke got to do with us? With tonight?"

"The way you treated her," Sheila said, suddenly feeling shy. "When I stopped the two of you in the alley behind the opera house and you had to leave her, you were such a nice guy to her. I just— I don't know. I wanted to be treated the way you treated her, I guess. With respect, but— like she needed to be taken care of, too."

"Believe me, Elke doesn't need to be taken care of."

"Neither do I. But sometimes..."

"I know," Max murmured, at last pulling Sheila free of her sweater. He slid his hands along her ribs, drawing her against him once more. "I know what you mean."

His mouth felt hot on her bare shoulder, and Sheila shuddered with pleasure. Deftly he managed to unfasten her bra with one hand—the parting snap making a small sound that seemed intensely intimate. In another minute, Sheila's breasts were uncovered. She pulled Max down onto the bed and almost cried out when his lean frame curled with hers. They faced each other on their sides—kissing, caressing, exploring. One of his strong arms found its way around her body, and his other hand slid between her knees.

Their kisses were hot and hungry, growing more insistent with every passing heartbeat. Under her fingertips, Max's body felt lithe and powerful. Sheila unfastened his pants and pushed them down to reach for the smooth, hard muscle beneath. Max groaned and fumbled hastily with the catch on her jeans. His clumsy efforts soon got them giggling.

"Wait," Sheila gasped, laughing. "Don't tear my clothes!"

"Then tear them yourself, woman," Max panted. "Need I remind you that you've already had the pleasure of seeing my splendid form?"

"And splendid it is."

He gave up on her jeans and captured her breasts instead—one with his mouth, the other with his gentle fingers. Both nipples were already hard peaks, but his caress pushed Sheila higher up the scale of excitement until she quivered with desire. She jerked off her jeans in record time, kicking her boots to the floor and finally seizing Max's hair in her hands before he drove her over the edge of ecstasy with his clever mouth and fingertips.

"Max, you're driving me crazy."

He stroked her body, but it was the heat of his gaze that made every nerve ending come alive as he let it roam over her skin, her hair, her face. "I want you to be wild," he said. "But not scared. I want to touch you everywhere, Sheila, but I'm worried about you."

"Let me show you what I like best," she whispered. Slowly, she began to caress Max, starting with his mouth, his neck, his chest. She pushed him over onto his back and teased him with her lips, her tongue and fingertips. Straddling his muscular frame, she tantalized him until Max was groaning and laughing at the same time. He arched against her, but Sheila teasingly evaded him over and over.

"I won't risk getting pregnant, Max. But I'm not in the habit of carrying any kind of protection with me. Will we have to find another way of pleasing each other?"

"No way," Max gasped. "Do you think I'd settle for anything less than everything now that I've got you here?"

The problem was that Max didn't know if he had any kind of protection in his loft, so he spent a breathless five minutes ransacking his belongings to find something. Sheila sat on his bed and watched, laughing at his desperation—whether it was as intense as he pretended, she wasn't sure—and admiring his body as he moved in the firelight.

Watching him made Sheila even more anxious to touch him again. The sight of his aroused state was as tantalizing as any caress and filled Sheila with desire more fiery than she'd ever known. When at last he gave a triumphant shout, she was on the verge of calling him back to the bed and to hell with the consequences.

With trembling hands, she helped him deal with the practical matter, then drew him down against her body. "Now let's get reckless," she whispered.

It was more than reckless: it was wonderfully mindless, awesomely primal and breathtakingly erotic. It might have lasted fifteen minutes or fifteen hours, for time seemed to swirl in a haze of slick, arching, panting pleasure.

For a while she rode above him, then suddenly he was in command. They wrestled and growled, laughing one minute and crying out the next.

When at last Max sank into the velvet softness of Sheila's body and felt her clutch him hard around his shoulders, he prayed he could keep his head. But soon he realized his prayer didn't matter. Sheila responded wildly, with such passion that he let go, too, thrusting deeper and deeper into her body and her emotions. He heard her cry out again and again, her body convulsing around him. Her voice was beautifully hoarse as she called his name, sending Max over the edge of control.

With a primitive surge of energy, he coaxed her once more to the heights of pleasure. Then suddenly, uncannily, they were moving together—harmonizing, matching, bonding. The rhythm changed to a kind of soar, sending them both surging to a magical place—a wonderful, luminous place.

They drifted for an eternity, communing in ecstasy. Licked by firelight, they lay together in sated perfection.

Max didn't remember who moved first or why. But eventually they were both nestled under the bedclothes, not speaking but gazing uncertainly into each other's eyes. When had he ever undergone such a transforming experience? Looking into Sheila's fathomless green eyes, he saw that she was equally moved.

He made a joke—or maybe she did. It was feeble, but it didn't matter. They started talking again—soft murmurings that made little sense, perhaps, but it was the tone of their voices, the tentative touches that were important.

Hunger eventually invaded their cocoon, sending Max to the telephone to call a Chinese restaurant that delivered. He went to the door wrapped in his bathrobe and came back to the bed with the bags to find Sheila feeling more amorous than hungry. They made love again, then with chopsticks fed each other the spicy food from the cardboard containers.

After eating, they showered together, then climbed back into bed and fell instantly asleep in each other's arms.

In the middle of the night, Max woke up. He lay in the darkness with Sheila's slender body curled against him, her head nestled on his shoulder, and her hair streaming across his chest and arms. She breathed gently, stirring a little as she slept.

Max found himself wondering what Sheila Malone dreamed about. Attackers who threatened women with guns? Brutes who beat up their wives and children? Burglaries? Break-ins?

Smiling in the darkness, Max decided that he wanted to give Sheila something else to dream about. Barely waking her, he made love to Sheila once more—a dreamy kind of love that made her smile as she dozed off to sleep again.

Seven

In the morning, the bed was as warm as buttered toast, making Sheila's aching muscles feel well-used and happy. She stretched tentatively, trying not to wake Max, though she decided it would only be fair. How many times had he wakened her during the night? Dozens? Or had she dreamed a few of those wonderful tussles?

With a smile, Sheila slid out of bed and stealthily scooped up her clothes. She dressed noiselessly in the bathroom, washed her face and gave up trying to untangle her hair.

Time to go. When she tiptoed out of the bathroom, though, Max groaned.

He rolled over on his stomach and peered at her from under the pillow he had jammed over his head. "What are you doing?"

"I have to go to work," she whispered.

"In the middle of the night?"

"It's morning."

Max threw off the pillow and squinted at the bedside clock. "It's not even six-thirty!"

"I go on duty at seven. Day shift this week."

"That's barbaric."

Sheila plunked onto the edge of the bed to pull on her boots. "It's the real world, hotshot."

He rolled over and linked his hands behind his head to look at her. His dark eyes were heavy lidded, and his mouth curved into a lazy smile. "If this is the real world, I like it a lot."

Sheila liked the way the bedclothes were tangled around his hips. His chest looked even more inviting than before. Noting a couple of tiny scratch marks on his shoulders, she felt herself turn a bit pink. She bent to yank on her boot. "It's freezing in here, you know. Don't you have a furnace?"

"Nope. It's plenty warm where I am. You could climb back in here and let me ward off the cold."

"Forget it." Sheila laughed. "I've got to go."

Max kicked off the covers. "I'll make you a cup of coffee first. That's the least I can do."

"No, no. Stay in bed. You'll give me something to fantasize about today."

He kissed her hard on the mouth. "I think you have plenty of fantasizing material already."

"True, true."

More content than she'd felt in a long time, Sheila finished dressing and watched Max saunter around the bed, stretching his arms as he went. He was a magnificent specimen of the male animal, and for a second Sheila was tempted to rip off her clothes again and go after him. Then he grabbed his luxurious bathrobe from the bedpost and spoiled her plan.

As he wrapped the garment around himself and headed for the kitchen, Sheila controlled her impulse to tackle him and tried instead to comb the tangles from her hair with her fingers.

"There's a brush in my suitcase over there," Max called out, noticing her trouble when he snapped on the kitchen light. "You're welcome to borrow it."

Sheila got to her feet and went over to the corner where a few bits of furniture were still piled. Max's luggage lay on the desk.

"I haven't had time to unpack," he said from the kitchen, yawning like a waking tiger. "Can you find it?"

"Yep." Sheila located his hairbrush and began to use it on her tumbled curls. As she brushed, she idly began to look at the furniture that had been jammed together in the corner. The desk was particularly handsome—an oak roll-top model that must have weighed half a ton.

"Where'd all this furniture come from?" Sheila asked.

"My father's apartment, most of it. And some from his office at the brewery."

"This desk is beautiful."

"The rolltop? I hate it. I slammed my fingers in it when I was a kid. Someday I may use the damn thing for firewood."

"You could sell it."

Over the sound of running water, he replied, "I'll probably give it to the Salvation Army when I'm finished with it."

Sheila tried one of the desk drawers. "Finished with it?" she repeated. "What are you doing?"

"I have to check through all that junk to make sure I've got all my father's business records straight—and to make sure he didn't leave anything of value."

Sheila's next question died in her throat. She had managed to tug open the smallest drawer and found herself looking at a revolver. It was an old piece—a Luger from World War II was her best guess—with an inlaid pearl handle that caught what little light was starting to glow in the tall windows. It was surrounded by bits of junk—paper clips, dull pencils, an old stapler.

Her first impulse was to ask Max about the gun. But something prevented her—cop's instinct, she supposed.

She glanced at Max and saw that he was finishing with the coffee and taking no notice of what she was doing. Cautiously Sheila touched the gun with her forefinger. Moving it aside, she saw something else beneath the gun: a ring. Judging by its size, it was a man's pinkie ring—a large diamond set in an oval onyx.

"Okay," said Max, coming up behind her. "Coffee in five minutes. You can wait that long, can't you?"

Sheila closed the drawer hastily and turned around. "Sure. I have five minutes. Aren't you cold?"

"The sight of you makes me warm enough." He took the hairbrush from Sheila's hand. "Let me do that."

His technique wasn't terribly efficient, but definitely sensual. Max brushed her hair lightly, then stroked each strand with his hand afterward. Sheila closed her eyes, remembering his stroke on other parts of her body. To prevent herself from asking him to go back to bed, she asked, "What have you found in the furniture, so far?"

"No priceless family heirlooms, if that's what you mean," replied Max, slipping his hand around her waist to snare her against him. He felt hard and deliciously masculine. "Mostly I've been looking for business-related paperwork. The deeds to these buildings, for instance, and some records about employees. I have to get things ready to open the brewery again."

"When will that happen?"

"In six months—at least that's my goal." He nuzzled her throat, making Sheila tingle all over. "Why are we talking about this when I'd rather be making love with you again?"

"I can't, Max. I have to go—"

He twisted her around in his arms, pulling Sheila flush with his body. His mouth found hers, silencing her weak protest. The kiss was warm and dizzying, and Sheila found herself winding her arms around his shoulders and pressing herself against the spot where it was impossible for his bathrobe to conceal his desire for her. Teasingly Max's tongue traced the shape of her teeth. He moved his hips in a slow, tantalizing rhythm that was hard not to mimic.

At last Sheila pulled away, breathless and shaken by how easily her body responded to his. "Don't tempt me, please, Max. I have to go."

"Will you be back?"

She couldn't look at him for a second, and a funny silence followed. Sheila wasn't sure what to say—there were so many factors to consider. Max's connection with the Pletheridge business, for one thing. Sheila knew she shouldn't plan on a relationship with a man like him, but now there was last night to consider. Her heart and her brain disagreed.

Max used one finger to lift her chin higher. His eyes were suddenly intense and his voice hardened. "Will you be back?"

"I don't know," she answered, meeting his gaze honestly.

He cursed. "Sheila, last night—"

"I know all about last night. I just can't make a commitment yet. And neither can you."

He didn't respond, except to tighten his grip on her, so Sheila said, "Let's not go looking for trouble, Max."

By his expression she could see that Max had more to say on the subject, but he chose to be cautious. His frown melted into a sexy grin, and he told her huskily. "I'm just looking for another night like last night."

Sheila was glad he could smile. "There could never be another night like last night."

"Just wait twelve hours, lady. When I get my strength back, I'll have you begging for mercy."

"Didn't I do that already?"

"As I recall, you were begging for more."

"See here—!" she started hotly.

"I love it when you blush," he murmured, holding her tightly against his near-naked frame. "I'm glad we had last night, Sheila. It was good to see you acting like your real self."

She slanted a look up at him. "How do you know what my real self is like?"

"I can read you like a book," Max replied cheerfully. "Just the way you read me."

I wish your printing was a little more legible, Sheila almost said. But she decided to kiss him instead, which was a mistake, because he almost had her sweater off a few minutes later, and then it was too late to have a cup of coffee before she dashed for the door.

"I'll get dressed and drive you to work," Max offered when she finally wiggled out of his embrace.

"No!" The last thing Sheila wanted to do was to drive up to the front door of the precinct house in Max Bollinger's Jaguar. She managed to sound polite. "No, thanks, I mean. I need some fresh air to clear my head and some clean clothes. I'll walk home."

"I'll call you," promised Max, when they parted at the door with a final kiss. "We'll send out for Italian food tonight."

Sheila wasn't ready to commit to another night—yet—but she replied, "Pasta's too messy to eat in bed."

He grinned. "We'll improvise."

Seeing Sheila dash down the stairs by morning light was the best sight Max had seen in a long time. She looked energized and happy, her bright hair flying out behind, and her green eyes glinting mischievously up at him when she turned at the bottom of the stairs to blow a kiss.

When she was out of sight, Max closed the door and leaned on it. For several minutes, he let the memory of their night together linger.

But at last, he said to himself, "Now what have you done, you idiot?"

Things were getting too complicated. He sighed. "It's time to settle matters for yourself before she finds out on her own."

Max crossed the loft to get dressed and get started. He had a lot of work to do before nightfall. When Sheila returned, he wanted to be able to tell her everything.

In the squad room an hour later, Cowboy was pacing like a madman when Sheila arrived.

"Dammit, Malone, where the hell have you been? I called your apartment three hours ago *and* your old man's place and—just where the hell did you spend the night?"

"What are you, my mother?" Sheila snapped back. "I have to tell you my every move?"

"I *needed* you, dammit. How am I supposed to—"

"Okay, okay. What's happened?" Sheila asked, determined to cut off Cowboy's interrogation before she had to reveal where she'd spent the night. "What's got you acting like a panicked bridegroom?"

"All hell broke loose last night, that's what's going on." Cowboy flung himself into another spate of pacing, his raincoat flapping, his cigar producing clouds of noxious smoke. He gestured with a coffee cup as he spoke, sloshing cold coffee on the floor. "About two in the morning, I got a call at home from the guys at the Third. They told me they'd found a stiff, so I went—"

"What stiff?"

"Shut up and listen. Cops from the Third Precinct were working on the Pletheridge case and guess what—they came up with Enrique!"

"What?"

Cowboy slammed his coffee cup down on the desk, splashing coffee everywhere. "Enrique Furmire! The loan shark, remember? You won't believe it, Malone. They found Furmire buried in the Pletheridge rose garden!"

Sheila sat down in the nearest chair. Suddenly she couldn't breathe, and she could barely make sense of Cowboy's rushed explanation.

"The other cops were checking out some tracks in the garden, see, hoping to pin the jewelry thing on somebody in the family. They had some tracking dogs snooping around outside in the garden—you should see the garden, Malone, it's freaking Versailles in that backyard. Anyway, the dogs went nuts."

"Over what?"

"The cops couldn't figure it out—why the dogs were digging in the ground instead of sniffing footprints. Finally the guy in charge says, 'Let's take a look,' so they got a couple of spades from the garage and half an hour later they're hitting Enrique's moldering bones!"

"H-how did they know it was Enrique?"

"Because he always wore a ton of jewelry—necklaces, rings, fancy watch—all that stuff. He had his name *engraved* on some of it!"

"He still had on his jewelry?"

"And not much else. He's been underground a couple of years, at least, wrapped in some rags or an old coat or something."

"What—why is he buried in the Pletheridge rose garden?"

"You idiot, because Max Bollinger put him there!"

Sheila gripped the edge of the desk to keep herself from leaping to her feet and screaming. But she didn't want to look like a fool. Not now. Not here. She sat still and tried to think, tried to force her brain to function logically.

Gulping back her first response, she managed to ask calmly, "Why would Max bury a body in the garden of a house where he doesn't live?"

Cowboy stopped pacing. "What?"

Sheila took a deep breath. "Max Bollinger hasn't ever lived in the Pletheridge house. He stayed there a few times when he was a kid, but he never actually lived there. Why would—"

"How do you know that?"

Sheila stared at her partner, knowing she had to come up with a plausible story or get him off the track with an emotional outburst. "Do I hit you with twenty questions every time you come up with something useful? Since when do you get off treating me like the junior partner here? I tell you, Max never lived in that house!"

"Max?" Cowboy repeated, coming to stand above her. His usual hound-dog expression looked very curious suddenly. "What's going on, Sheila?"

"Nothing. Tell me what else is going on here. You've got your coat on."

Cowboy stubbed out his cigar and started to button his raincoat. "We're going for a ride."

"Why?"

"We're going downtown to get a preliminary autopsy report. It was a slow night, so they rushed Furmire through. The creep's family is supposed to be down there, too, so we can talk to them."

"About what?" Sheila demanded, though she was already following her partner down the stairs. "What is the family going to tell us?"

It turned out that the family had a lot to tell them. And none of it was information that Sheila enjoyed hearing.

His wife, a noisy woman the size of a walrus, was wailing and bawling so loudly that they heard her before they reached the basement where the city morgue and the medical examiner's office were.

"My dear husband!" the woman shrieked. "He is dead! Dead!"

"Ma," said her son, a pimple-faced teenager with a temperament as laid-back as his mother's was hyper. "He's been dead four years. Why all the waterworks?"

"He's gone!" The woman hiccuped. "Gone to the angels!"

"Not exactly the angels," Cowboy muttered under his breath. "Hello, ma'am, I'm Detective Stankowsky, and this is Detective Malone. We're wondering if you can tell us anything about your husband's disappearance."

"He is gone!" she wailed again.

Sheila looked at her son. "Have you learned anything yet?"

The kid shrugged, digging a crumpled pack of cigarettes from the pocket of his grubby ski jacket. "He was scum. He was going to die anyway."

That sent Mrs. Furmire into a tirade against her son, but she soon collapsed on a wooden bench and began to weep as though her heart were broken.

The kid said, "The cops gave us a look at his stuff—the necklaces, you know. There ain't no body to identify."

"And the necklaces definitely belong to your father?"

"Yeah." The boy lit a cigarette and blew smoke. He jerked his head toward his mother. "She's upset 'cause one of the rings is missing."

"A ring?" Cowboy repeated. "What's the big deal?"

"It had a diamond in it. A big one." The kid looked at his mother, crumpled in a sniffling heap. "She was hoping to get the ring back so she could sell it. She needs some money. The old man didn't leave her nothing. Not in *his* business."

Sheila could scarcely make her voice work. "What kind of ring was it?"

"Gold with a black setting and this big rock in the middle. A pinkie ring. You know."

"Yes," Sheila answered softly. "I think I know."

Was it possible? Had she seen Enrique Furmire's ring in the desk Max had in his loft?

Without noticing Sheila's reaction to the news, Cowboy told her, "Let's go see who we can talk to."

They pushed through a pair of double doors marked City Morgue and cut left into the immaculate hallway of the medical examiner's office. The heavy scent of cleaning fluids and heaven only knew what other kinds of chemicals hung in the air.

Cowboy shivered in his raincoat. "I hate this place."

"It's not exactly my favorite hangout," Sheila replied, not looking into any of the open doorways for fear of laying eyes on a corpse.

They found the medical examiner in his office smoking a cigar. All the men who worked in the morgue favored smelly stogies, and the women smoked cigarettes. The M.E. was Dr. Philip Tong, a classical music lover who played

Mozart on a set of headphones all the time. He spotted Cowboy and Sheila in the doorway of his office and popped off the headset.

He snapped his fingers. "Stankowsky and Mallory, right?"

"Malone," Sheila corrected. "Do you have any news for us on Enrique Furmire?"

The medical examiner had a lot of technical mumbo-jumbo to report, but finally cut to the cause of death.

"He was shot," Dr. Tong explained. "I can't tell what kind of gun at this point or even whether or not the gunshot actually killed him. Because there's so little flesh left on the bones, we haven't very much to go on."

"This gives us enough to start our work," Cowboy said. "You'll give us a jingle if you learn something else?"

Tong slipped his headphones back into place. "Sure thing. See you around, Stankowsky. You, too, Mallory."

Sheila didn't bother to correct him. Outside, she said to her partner, "How come he knows your name and not mine?"

Cowboy shrugged. "It pays to get your face recognized. I've been campaigning a little."

"You really want that promotion to Homicide, don't you?"

"You betcha," he answered.

It was obvious that Cowboy intended to use the Pleth-eridge-Bollinger situation to get himself a promotion. Sheila shivered, knowing how determined her partner could be. Cowboy was going to solve the Furmire case, no matter what.

In the car he was full of theories, but Sheila listened with only half an ear as she drove back to the precinct house. She knew Max couldn't have killed Enrique Furmire. He wasn't capable of murder. Over and over, she told herself so.

But Cowboy was bound and determined to prove that Max *was* a killer.

"What's the matter with you?" Cowboy asked abruptly, breaking off his theorizing. "Your hands are shaking."

"What? They are not!" She gripped the steering wheel tighter. "I'm thinking, that's all."

"About Bollinger?"

"Why would I be thinking about him? Can't a girl let her mind wander a little without being accused of—"

"Take it easy," Cowboy soothed. "Boy, you've got a bee in your bonnet this morning."

"I got up on the wrong side of the bed."

"Yeah," snorted Cowboy. "But the question is whose bed was it?"

Sheila hit the brakes and yanked the car over onto the nearest sidewalk. Cowboy cursed as he was thrown against the dashboard.

"What are you trying to do, kill me?"

"I'm getting out," Sheila snapped. "You can drive yourself wherever the hell you want to go!"

"Jeez, Sheila, I didn't mean—"

"I don't care what you meant, and I don't want to hear any apologies, all right? I just want some fresh air."

"Sheila, please—"

She unsnapped her seat belt and popped open the door. "I'll get back to the precinct when I feel like it."

"Okay, okay," said Cowboy. "But take my beeper, all right? Please, I've got to make sure you're not over the edge—"

"I'm not going to do anything stupid!" Sheila grabbed the beeper and shoved it into her pocket.

"I know you won't. You're okay, Malone. But take the day off, why don't you? You could use a vacation."

"Go to hell," she snarled, slamming the door behind her.

She stuffed her hands into the pockets of her jacket and stormed up the sidewalk as fast as she could. Cowboy drove past and waved tentatively at her, but she didn't wave back. When he was out of sight, she spotted a trolley stopping at the next corner. She ran down the sidewalk and jumped on for a ride into the South Side. She got off on Carson Street and looked for a telephone booth.

The operator had two new phone numbers under Max's name. Sheila punched in the number of his loft apartment, and Max picked up the phone on the first ring.

"It's me," Sheila said shortly. "Are you alone?"

"Unfortunately, yes," replied Max, sounding pleased to hear her voice. "A beautiful woman spent the night in my arms, but she had to leave at an ungodly hour."

"I need to see you, Max."

He laughed. "Darling, you're insatiable. Phone sex won't do, huh? Okay, how about a lunch break?"

"I'm not talking about a friendly meeting. This is police business."

"Haven't all our meetings been police business, after a fashion?"

"Dammit, Max, I'm not kidding around. I need to see you immediately. And it's got to be at your loft."

"Okay," he agreed, sounding curious. "I'll be here."

Sheila walked seven blocks to the brewery and found the door to his garage unlocked. She went up the stairs and knocked on his door. When Max called out, she pushed through. Max was sitting on a stool at the kitchen counter, reading from a sheaf of papers.

She was surprised to see him wearing a pair of horn-rimmed reading glasses. Max looked sexier than ever—his hair still wet from the shower, his face freshly shaved. That, combined with the speed with which she'd climbed the stairs, resulted in Sheila being unable to speak.

With a grin Max got up from his chair and came around the desk, taking Sheila by her shoulders and swooping down to kiss her. Sheila blocked the kiss and gave him a deadly look.

"Wow," he remarked. "What's happened?"

"Plenty," said Sheila, still breathing hard. "And none of it makes you look like a saint, Mr. Bollinger."

"What are you talking about?"

"Last night, some cops from your mother's neighborhood dug up a body in her rose garden."

If Max already knew about Enrique Furmire's final resting place, he made an excellent job of looking surprised. His hands froze on her shoulders. "What kind of body? You mean a *person*?"

"That's questionable," Sheila snapped, breaking out of his embrace, "since not everyone considered Enrique Furmire to be a human being."

"Furmire! *He's* buried at my mother's place? Why?"

"I was hoping," she said, turning around to watch Max's face, "that you could tell me."

Max blinked and a long moment passed before he spoke. "You think I know something about this?"

"The house belongs to your mother. Furmire and your father weren't seeing eye to eye. Furmire died just before you left for Germany. And this morning, I couldn't help noticing a ring in the drawer of that desk over there."

Max frowned. "A ring? Where?"

Sheila led him across the floor to the pile of furniture. She opened the rolltop desk and yanked out the small drawer. The gun lay in full view, and under that rattled the diamond pinkie ring.

Max reached for the ring and held it up to the windows. "Okay, it's a ring. What's it got to do with anything?"

"I bet it's Enrique Furmire's diamond pinkie ring," Sheila said. "It's the only piece of jewelry he normally wore that wasn't found on his body this morning. I want to know, Max, what the hell it's doing here."

She wanted him to tell her he was innocent—that he knew nothing about Enrique Furmire's death. Sheila stood there holding her breath, watching his face and praying he could vindicate himself.

He didn't. His expression was enough to tell Sheila that he wasn't lily white.

Max caught her hand and placed the ring into her palm. "I haven't the faintest idea where this ring came from."

But his expression said something else.

Sheila asked, "Where did you get the desk? You said it belonged to your father."

"Look," he began, "I can't be sure—"

"Whose gun is that?"

"Sheila, I got this furniture out of storage, and I haven't gone through all of it yet. I started with the file cabinets, so I can't tell you what's in all of these drawers. The gun could be anyone's—"

"Your father's?"

"Maybe."

"Have you touched it?"

"Not lately."

Sheila steeled herself to ask, "What about four years ago?"

Max's gaze turned as cold as stone. "Are you asking me if I killed somebody with that gun?"

"I have to ask, Max. It's my job." Talking too fast, Sheila hurried on. "What's this gun doing here? Is it yours?"

A tense muscle jumped in his jaw. "You shouldn't have to ask me a question like that, Sheila."

"I've known you for a week, Max. That's hardly long enough to make any critical judgments!"

"We've put that week to good use," he retorted. "Last night—"

Sheila cut him off. Turning away, she said, "Last night was a mistake. I see that clearly now. I should have waited until I was sure about you."

"It was not a mistake!" Max grabbed her arm and prevented Sheila from tearing free. "We both needed to cut loose for once, and thank heaven we did it together. I don't regret it for a minute."

"Your job doesn't depend on using your head the way mine does. How am I supposed to tell my partner about this ring without letting him guess what happened last night?"

"So what if he finds out? I'm not worried."

"Of course you're not! *I'm* the one who's supposed to be above reproach. I'm playing with fire here, Max, and I'm going to get burned. How badly is the next question."

He let go of her arm so forcefully that Sheila staggered back against the kitchen counter. His voice was deadly quiet. "You don't trust me even yet, do you?"

"I can't afford to!" Sheila cried. "I'm paid to keep the public safe, Max. I took an oath! If you're a criminal, it's my sworn duty to bring you to justice."

"Justice!" Max blew his stack. "Whose justice? When you shot that guy last week, was that justice? You made a snap decision!"

"Somebody has to make those snap decisions, dammit—that's why cops were invented. You can't go around breaking rules when you feel like it! In no time, we'd have complete anarchy! Now, tell me what you know, Max. Tell me so I can help, for God's sake."

He turned away. "Sheila—"

"What's going on?"

"Let me find out for myself," he said suddenly, keeping his back turned so she couldn't see his face. "Let me finish looking through my father's things."

"What do you expect to find?"

"I don't know—something that will help me put the pieces together."

"How do I know you're not just covering your own tracks?"

He wheeled around slowly. "You'll just have to trust me, I guess."

Sheila shook her head. "Don't put me in this spot, Max. I can't—"

He put his arms around her, hugging her hard against his body. "You can do anything you want, Sheila."

"Max, please—"

He kissed her before she could say anything else. His mouth came down quickly, but eased up at once, softening the kiss to a coaxing contact that was gentle and sexy at the same time. Sheila felt herself go all warm and buttery inside and she hated herself for being weak. Max passed his fingertips down her cheek, then brushed the peak of her breast through her sweater.

Sheila managed to wedge her hands against his chest and push. The kiss broke awkwardly, and Max tightened his grip to keep Sheila from wrenching out of his arms.

"Sheila—"

"Don't," she warned. "This is a cheap trick, and I don't like you for trying it."

"It's not a trick. It's simple attraction between two people who care about each other. I think you care a little about me, Sheila, or you wouldn't be here now like this. You could have come with a squad car and handcuffs, but—"

"Max, tell me what you know!" She seized his shirt in her hands. "Tell me, dammit!"

"I can't. Not at the expense of people I love."

Sheila stared up at him. "Then there *is* something going on?"

Max had no chance to answer. They were interrupted by a shrill beeping that suddenly emanated from the device in Sheila's pocket. Max released her instinctively, and she dug the beeper out of her pocket. She hit the switch and listened to the dispatcher, who reeled off a telephone number.

Without saying a word to Max, Sheila reached across his counter for the telephone. She dialed the number, and was put through to Cowboy immediately.

"Where the hell are you?" he demanded.

"Is that why you paged me? To find out where I am?"

"Just so you're not jumping off a bridge someplace. You better get back here. Something just turned up."

"What?"

"A bullet. The crew working at the Pletheridge house found a bullet in the same hole they brought Enrique out of. Ballistics just called with an ID on the gun used."

"So tell me now."

"It was a Luger. A—"

Sheila cursed.

"What's wrong?" Cowboy's voice sharpened. "Where the hell are you, partner? Do you know something about this gun?"

Sheila blew a sigh. "Yeah, maybe I do."

Cowboy let out a string of colorful expletives. "Where? How? Do you have it?"

If she told Cowboy about the gun, Max would be in jail before lunch. Sheila wasn't ready for that—she wasn't convinced Max knew anything about Enrique Furmire.

Between a rock and a hard place, Sheila knew it was time to start working solo until she got solid evidence that would either clear Max or put him away.

Where to start? Max was watching her unabashedly from across the counter, his face immobile. In his eyes, however, Sheila read a stubborn refusal and knew he wasn't going to help her. There was only one place she could begin her investigation, and that was at the beginning, at the moment she'd first learned of the case—the Pletheridge break-in.

"Cowboy," she said suddenly. "Tell me what hockshop took the jewelry."

"From the Pletheridge dame? The guys downtown already checked that out—"

"Just tell me!"

Her partner growled in frustration. "Swanky's on Mulberry. Do you want to meet me there?"

"No," she answered quickly. "Just—"

"Malone," her partner demanded sternly, "what are you up to? Have you got something going you're not telling me about? Something with that Bollinger guy?"

"Forget it, Cowboy—"

"I mean it, Malone, you better watch your step. Don't let a handsome face lead you into trouble."

Trouble isn't a strong enough word for what I'm in Sheila thought, but said, "Don't worry about me."

"I *will* worry, especially if you've gone soft on Bollinger. That's not what's happening, is it? Because you know better, Malone."

"Cowboy—"

"Don't let your feelings blind you to the facts. Stay away from him, Malone. Let me handle the case."

"I can't," Sheila said, and hung up softly.

Max didn't speak again. It was clear he had nothing more to say. Sheila left his loft, wondering if it was the last time she'd ever see him—as a free man.

Eight

Sheila walked to her apartment to get her own car and drove across town to Swanky's Hock Shop, a place she visited from time to time on police business. Swanky's was known as a relatively clean shop, since Swanky made it a point not to take in stolen goods if he could help it.

Swanky himself talked to Sheila. "Yeah, I remember that stuff. It was ordinary jewelry—a little silver and gold, but nothing real expensive. No diamonds or pearls or nothin'."

"Do you remember the person who brought it in?"

"Sure. I told the other cops about this. It was a young guy, see? Between twenty and thirty."

"About thirty-five?"

"No. Younger, I'd say."

Not Max, surely, Sheila thought. Max looked closer to forty than twenty. Still, maybe Swanky wasn't a good judge. "Can you remember anything else about him?"

Swanky scratched his stomach. He was wearing a Pitts-
burgh Steelers football shirt with the number thirty-two
starting to peel off from old age, certainly not from too
many launderings. "I dunno. I'm not good at this stuff. He
was a good-looking kid, that's what I remember."

"Coloring?"

"Couldn't tell. He had on a hat and—"

"What kind of hat? You mean a ski cap, or what?"

Swanky grinned, highly amused. "A fedora—a real
pretty one, too. The kid wore it cocked off to one side like
he thought he was Humphrey Bogart or something."

Intrigued, Sheila asked, "What else was he wearing?"

Swanky shrugged. "Some kind of big coat—a modern
one with lots of style like you see in magazines. The kid
looked good, I have to tell you. That's why I figured he was
okay."

"How did he act?"

"Real cocky and smartass. Like he was doing me a favor. He got a shock when I told him the stuff was worth
only a couple hundred bucks—"

"So he'd never done this kind of thing before?"

"Right. He was wet behind the ears, but didn't know it."

Sheila suddenly knew exactly who Swanky was describ-
ing. She was sure the man who had brought the jewelry into
the hockshop was none other than Cameron Pletheridge.
No doubt the guys at the Third Precinct would come to the
same conclusion, soon. Sheila had the added advantage of
having met Cameron at Max's office. Maybe the other cops
hadn't been able to track him down yet.

But why would Cameron steal his mother's jewelry and
hock it? Why not just ask her for money?

She recalled the conversation she'd overheard between
Max and his younger brother. The gist of it had been about

Cameron's lack of funds and how he couldn't get any more from their mother.

A thought struck Sheila. It wasn't uncommon for people to fake a break-in so they could report their missing heirlooms to their insurance companies to get their hands on some cash. Had Cameron decided to steal the jewelry so he could have both the cash from hocking the stuff as well as insurance money?

That might explain why the job was done so amateurishly. No self-respecting thief would hock the jewelry in the same town where he'd stolen it.

Sheila thanked Swanky, who patted her hand and said, "I like you, little girl. You come and see me again sometime, you hear? Just for a social visit, maybe."

Sheila laughed and said she'd be back in a couple of hours, and left Swanky grinning at his cash register.

It was time to let Cowboy in on what she had learned. He didn't believe her, at first.

"Cameron Pletheridge? Why would he steal his mother's jewelry? She's his meal ticket!"

"Things are going sour between them," Sheila argued. "So he took some of her jewelry and hocked it. Or maybe they're trying the old insurance scam together. Who knows? The point is, Swanky can probably identify Cameron. All we have to do is get a photo down there and let him decide."

Cowboy looked none too pleased with her theory. "You seem pretty damn anxious to prove Bollinger's innocence."

"He is innocent."

"I suppose you'd like me to believe he had nothing to do with the Furmire murder, too?"

"That's something else. We take this one case at a time, all right? We—you and me, partner. No more of this I-want-a-promotion garbage."

Cowboy was surprised. "You mad at me about that?"

"No," Sheila said brusquely. "Not exactly, that is."

Her partner touched her arm. "Hey, Malone, I don't want this to look like I want to dump you. You're the best. It's just . . ."

"Yeah?"

"Well, hell, you're going to finish law school pretty soon. I figured you planned to get off the force and hang a shingle downtown. You know—maybe you're not cut out for this job, Malone."

"I'm a cop, damn you! I'm not leaving the force until I'm ready to leave the force."

"Considering what happened last week—"

"I know what happened," she snapped. "And I'm not going to let it chase me into another line of work."

"Sheila, there's no shame in admitting you can't handle it."

"I *can* handle it!"

"You're trying too hard to prove you're okay. Look, you've got to relax again—and I'm not sure you can. You can't work when you're all tied up in knots inside, Sheila."

"I put this case together, didn't I? Before the guys over at the Third made everything fit."

"You haven't done it yet, either," Cowboy pointed out. "The whole Cameron Pletheridge idea is just a theory."

"Then come with me," Sheila urged. "Let's go over to the newspaper office and dig up a photo of Cameron. We'll take it to Swanky and see what he says. I think he'll prove we can pick up Cameron and put him in a lineup. Are you with me? Or are you scared I might spoil your chances for promotion?"

Her partner looked at her for a while and finally threw his pencil down. He reached for his coat. "Okay, Malone. You've got me on your side. Let's go."

After an hour of scrounging around, they found a photograph of Cameron Pletheridge in the archives of the newspaper office. It was a picture of Cameron dressed in a dinner jacket and squiring a lovely young lady to a charity ball. At Cowboy's suggestion, they took along a few other pictures of men approximately Cameron's height and coloring to give Swanky something to choose from. Sheila didn't mind Cowboy's prudence. It was good police procedure.

But she was exultant when Swanky picked out Cameron at once and planted his fat forefinger on Cameron's photo.

"That's the kid," Swanky said excitedly. "Real snotty, all right. He needs a kick in the pants."

"He'll get worse than that," Cowboy replied, gathering up the photos and putting his hand out to shake Sheila's. "Thanks to this detective's hard work, the kid is going to jail."

Sheila wasn't delighted to realize that she was going to get the credit for the arrest of Max's brother. Normally, she would have been enormously pleased to beat the cops at the Third Precinct to a bust. Even learning that they hadn't made much progress due to assigning the case a low-priority status in the face of a crime wave over the past couple of days, wasn't as depressing as wondering what Max's reaction was going to be.

Seeing Cameron Pletheridge in handcuffs later that afternoon did not make Sheila especially happy. Nor did seeing Max stride into the precinct house to bail Cameron out of jail.

Sheila's heart started to slam the minute she saw Max enter the squad room. A towering figure of rage, he halted in front of Sheila's desk. "What the hell is going on?"

She stood slowly, trying to keep her cool. "We've arrested your brother, Mr. Bollinger On suspicion of—"

"What for? Cameron wouldn't hurt a flea!"

"Fleas weren't involved," Sheila replied, struggling to remain professional. "It was mostly gold, actually."

He braced one fist on her desk and leaned close, his dark brows snapped down over his fiery eyes. "What are you talking about, Sheila?"

Cowboy hurried over to find out what was going on. "Anything I can help with, Malone?"

"Buzz off," Max snapped, not even glancing at Cowboy but keeping his gaze riveted on Sheila. "Explain to me why my brother's being framed."

"He's not being framed, Max," Sheila said. "In fact, he confessed already."

"*Confessed?* What did you do to make him do that?"

"Nothing at all. Cameron admits he took the jewelry, made it look like a burglary and hocked the stuff downtown."

"Jewelry?" Max looked truly startled. "A burglary?"

"Your mother's jewelry, of course. He stole it himself. He confessed already. You'll have to wait if you've come to post bail. He has to be arraigned and—"

Max cursed again, and straightened, passing one hand over his forehead.

Cowboy stepped between them as if to ward off an explosion of temper. "Cool down, Bollinger. Maybe you ought to start worrying about yourself, not your little brother."

"What the hell are you talking about?"

Cowboy thrust his face within inches of Max's. "We have a few questions we'd like to ask."

Max put his hand on Cowboy's chest to prevent the cop from bullying him into taking a pace backward. "Call my lawyer if you want to get talkative, pal."

"Why, you—"

"Cowboy, take it easy," Sheila interrupted sharply. "I have a feeling Mr. Bollinger is surprised we arrested his brother on the burglary charge."

"What?"

Max controlled his expression at once. "What's going on?"

"Maybe you can tell us," Sheila suggested. "You thought we arrested Cameron on another charge, didn't you?"

"Look," Max began, "I don't know exactly what's going on here. But I think I'd better come clean before things really get screwed up. I've got a few things to tell you."

"Oh, yeah?" Cowboy challenged. "Like what?"

"I found some things," Max said, reaching into the pocket of his bomber jacket. "I thought they might be helpful."

Sheila gasped as Max dropped the Luger on her desk. It clattered onto the blotter, spun on its chamber and came to a stop, gleaming under the fluorescent lights. Next came Enrique Furmire's diamond pinkie ring.

"I thought these might be useful to you," Max told them.

"Where did these things come from?" Cowboy demanded, seizing the ring and examining it.

"I found them in some furniture that belonged to my father."

"Furniture?"

"A desk, actually."

Cowboy stared at Max. "Wait a minute. How'd you know we were looking for these?"

Before Max concocted a lie to protect her, Sheila said, quietly, "I told him about the M.E.'s report, Cowboy."

Her partner swung on Sheila. "You *what*?"

"I forced her," Max interjected quickly. "She wasn't going to say a word, but I—"

"You don't have to cover for me," Sheila interrupted. "I made my own decisions."

Cowboy looked mystified. "What's going on here? Sheila, you're not—you two aren't—"

Sheila stood up. "Maybe it's time I went to see the lieutenant. I've got a few things I'd better straighten out."

"Sheila, don't," Max warned.

"Stay out of this, Max. I know what I'm doing. Come on, Cowboy. Let's go see Fiske."

"You can't," Cowboy ground out from between clenched teeth. "He's gone to lunch. Besides, I think your loyal partner ought to get the story first. Just what the hell has been going on?"

A few heads turned in the squad room, causing Max to say mildly, "Shouldn't we find a place that's a little more private?"

"Butt out of this, Bollinger. She's been my partner a hell of a lot longer than you've been in the picture. I want to know what you've been doing to her."

"What you should have been doing," Max shot back. "When she needed a friend, all you could do was—"

"Shut up, both of you," Sheila snapped. "What is this? You both think I'm a child who needs your protection? Wise up, boys! I've been my own person for a long time."

"You can take care of yourself," Max said, "but—"

"But nothing. There's the lieutenant now. C'mon, Cowboy. Let's go into his office. And you," she told Max, "should wait right here."

Sheila stalked into Lieutenant Fiske's office with Cowboy at her heels. He was red in the face and muttering as he closed the door behind them and proceeded to sulk while Sheila laid everything on the line for her superior officer.

Fiske listened impassively throughout the whole explanation. Then he burped and said wearily. "Why can't you people wait until I've digested my lunch before you dump your troubles on me?"

"I thought these troubles affected us all, sir," Sheila replied.

"You're right." Fiske clasped his hands together and leaned his elbows on his desk blotter. "We've got two cases that appear to be separate—the Pletheridge break-in, which is technically a case that belongs to another precinct, and the Furmire murder, which is four years old—but could have been committed by a man who has just returned to our precinct and may be a danger to society. Am I right?"

"Right," Sheila agreed cautiously.

"The two cases might be related—only because the players on the scorecard have the same mother."

"Right."

"Or they could be completely separate cases."

"Exactly."

Fiske turned to Cowboy. "Do we have any other suspects—other guys who could have killed Enrique Furmire?"

"Not yet," Cowboy responded. "Max Bollinger is the most likely. He left the country soon after Furmire disappeared. He is presently in possession of the murder weapon and the pinkie ring always worn by the victim."

"But he has voluntarily brought them to us," the lieutenant pointed out. "Is that the act of a guilty man?"

"Not usually, sir," Cowboy answered. "But—"

"But nothing," Fiske said. "Bring Bollinger in here, Malone, and we'll all talk to him."

Sheila got up and went out into the squad room to get Max.

But he wasn't there. Worse yet, the Luger was no longer on the desk where he'd dropped it. She cursed herself for not picking it up in the first place.

With her chest aching inside, Sheila returned to Fiske's office to say Max had bolted, and the lieutenant stood up from his desk.

"That," he declared, "is the act of a guilty man. Go pick him up for questioning, Detectives. I'll expect you back here in an hour."

Cowboy and Sheila left the precinct house together. Sheila could hardly speak, and Cowboy was hyperattuned to her mood. However, he couldn't find the right words to comfort her until they were pulling up in front of Max's loft entrance. Finally he decided he had to say something. He put his hand out to prevent Sheila from opening the door.

"Listen," he said. "I'm sorry about this, Malone. I can see this Bollinger guy means something to you."

"He doesn't."

"You've gone out of your way to protect him," Cowboy pointed out. "And you came right out and told the lieutenant you slept with the guy."

"I figured it was best to put all my cards on the table."

"Yeah, well...I know you enough to understand that you don't go to bed with just anybody, Malone. He's under your skin, isn't he?"

"A lot of good that will do if he ends up in jail."

"Do you think he's innocent?"

"I don't know what I believe anymore," Sheila answered, meaning it. "Why would he run out of the precinct house unless..."

"Unless he has something to hide."

She shook her head. "I don't know. Maybe I'm stupid these days. Maybe shooting that kid last week has messed up my radar."

"I don't think so," Cowboy said. "I think you're still a cop, Malone."

Sheila suddenly wanted to cry. If her partner had made a move to hug her, she would have done exactly that. But Cowboy didn't try any such thing. After all, he knew her better than most anybody. He gave her a friendly punch on the arm, which made Sheila's urge to break down evaporate immediately. Then they got out of the car, ready to do a job.

They tried Max's apartment first. No answer. Obviously he hadn't gone home after leaving the precinct house.

"Any ideas where he might be?" Cowboy asked.

"Let's try the brewery."

The brick building across the alley was unlocked, and the door was ajar, inviting entry. All the lights were blazing in the brewery.

"Looks like somebody's home," Cowboy commented softly as they slipped inside. "Anybody else working here besides Bollinger?"

"Not that I know of," Sheila replied, keeping her voice low. Then she demanded, "What are you doing?"

Cowboy had pulled his service revolver from inside his coat, and he was checking it quickly. "What does it look like I'm doing? Bollinger's got a gun, hasn't he? That makes him armed and maybe dangerous. And since he left the precinct house against your orders, I suspect the guy wants to avoid getting himself arrested. I don't know about you, but that makes me real nervous, partner.''

"He's not going to shoot us.''

"No?'' Cowboy looked at her quizzically. "Can you promise that?''

"N-no.''

"Then get out your gun, Malone. And it better be loaded this time.''

Unwillingly, Sheila drew her gun. Together they walked down the echoing corridor toward Max's office. Sheila's heart was racing. Cowboy called his name, but got no response. When they arrived in the office, it was empty. But the light had been left on, and Max's reading glasses lay across a stack of papers.

"He's been here,'' Cowboy observed quietly. "And recently. Feel this.''

A mug half filled with coffee sat on the desk by the papers, and when Sheila put her hand against it, the warmth of the cup radiated against her palm. Max had been there very recently.

"Okay,'' said Cowboy, "my guess is he's still in this building. I think we'll call for backup.''

"We can handle this ourselves, Cowboy.''

"But—''

"Unless you're scared I can't handle it.''

His voice turned singsong. "Sheila—''

"Come on,'' she urged aggressively, in no mood to be placated. "Let's check the place out.''

They split up at the end of the corridor—Cowboy going into the cavernous brewery and Sheila taking the rest of the offices one at a time. When she was almost finished, the lights went out.

Sheila stood in the middle of one empty office and tried not to tremble. She could hear Cowboy yelling in the brewery—calling for Max at first, then to her to make sure she was okay. Sheila didn't answer. She let her eyes get accustomed to the darkness.

Then she heard footsteps.

With her heart in her throat, Sheila listened. She slipped noiselessly to the open door and waited, straining to see in the half-light.

Max came into view—striding down the long corridor alone. When he came even with the open office door, Sheila stepped out into his path.

She had her gun drawn, and that was the first thing Max saw. He stopped short.

Sheila said, "You don't look surprised to see me, Max."

"I figured you'd come," he answered, drawing a breath and glancing over her shoulder. "Where's your partner?"

"Nearby," Sheila replied, trying to steady the gun in her hand. "Max, we need to take you back to the precinct house. Lieutenant Fiske wants to talk to you."

"I can't," Max said softly. "I have something to do first."

He moved to cut around her, so Sheila had to raise the barrel of her revolver to stop him.

"Hold it, Max. I mean it. You have to come with me."

"I'm sorry, Sheila. I need a little more time."

"I can't just let you go!"

"Yes, you can."

"Dammit, Max, I'm a police officer. If you resist arrest, I can—"

"Is that what I'm doing? Resisting arrest? I thought you just wanted me for questioning?"

"Same thing. This situation boils down to me being the boss and you doing exactly what I say. And I want you to come with me."

Steadily, Max demanded, "And what will you do if I don't?"

The gun in Sheila's hand felt as heavy as twenty pounds of lead. Her voice was shaky when she urged, "Don't do this to me, Max. Please cooperate."

He looked amused for a second. "Do you say please to all the criminals you come across?"

"Max—"

He lifted his head as Cowboy's voice shouted for her—a little closer this time. The sound had a galvanizing effect on Max. He said, "I'm sorry, Sheila. I've got to go before your partner gets here."

He started to move around her again. Sheila cried, "Max!"

"I'll explain later—when I can prove what I believe. Until then—"

"Stop, Max. Stop right where you are."

He disobeyed, backing away from her in the direction of the open double doors. "I'll call you," he told her.

"Max, stop or I'll shoot."

"You won't shoot me," he replied, giving her a quick smile. "We've been lovers."

"I'm a cop, Max."

"But a woman first. And a woman I think I've fallen in love with."

"Don't play games with me."

"It's not a game. I love you, Sheila. And I want us to be together. Which means I've got business to take care of first. So I have to go."

"We can take care of business together. Let us help."

"I have to do this alone. Goodbye, love. I'll catch up with you in a couple of hours."

"*No*, Max."

"See you soon."

Sheila pulled the trigger.

The explosion sounded like a bomb blast. The recoil of the gun felt like a kick in the shoulder, but Sheila absorbed it and then trained the nose of her weapon on Max's chest. He flinched as the first bullet whanged off the open door and whined into the distance. His face registered complete shock.

"I'm very good on the practice range, Max," Sheila warned. "I can put a bullet wherever I want to."

"I believe you." Max raised his hands over his head. "It's okay. I'm not going anywhere."

Cowboy skidded around the corner in the dark, his gun in hand. He looked terrified. "Sheila! I heard— Are you okay?"

Sheila felt as if her entire bloodstream had turned to ice. Her limbs throbbed, and her head was suddenly very light. She sagged against the wall, more frightened than she could ever remember having been before. But she didn't drop her gun. It was still steady in her hand.

"I'm sorry," Max apologized. "I should have realized."

Sheila didn't answer. She couldn't speak. Instead she let Cowboy take over, and she went to the telephone in Max's office to call for belated backup. Then she sat in Max's swivel chair and put her head in her hands.

Then she cried.

Nine

Reporters must have gotten wind of the story, because when the two uniformed cops grabbed Max by his shoulders and hustled him out of a very uncomfortable squad car with his wrists handcuffed behind his back, half the journalists in town were jostling each other on the steps of the precinct house. Max was tempted to tell them all to go to hell, but that wasn't going to help. He allowed the cops to lead him indoors, but he was seething inside.

Sheila was nowhere to be seen.

"Where's Detective Malone?" was his first question to Lieutenant Fiske, who appeared in the airless interrogation room where Max waited under the watchful eyes of his uniformed escorts. "Is she all right?"

"Detective Malone is in good hands," replied Fiske, using a key to unfasten the cuffs from Max's wrists. "Now, if we could get down to matters at hand—"

"I need to see her."

Fiske's face tightened, as if Max had suggested something entirely distasteful. Then he handed the cuffs and key to one of the cops, relaxed his expression and pretended Max hadn't spoken. "Tell me, Mr. Bollinger, have you called a lawyer?"

"I don't give a damn about a lawyer." Max massaged his wrists to get the feeling back. "I need to see Sheila."

"I don't think that's necessary."

The door opened then, breaking off their conversation. Fiske looked annoyed when he saw who was standing in the hall. "Ah. Here she is anyway."

Sheila and her partner were allowed into the small interrogation room by a third uniformed cop who was guarding the door. Max saw at once how pale Sheila was, but her chin looked as stubborn as ever. Her eyes were coolly steady when they met his.

He longed to tell her a lot of things—and apologize for the stupid way he'd behaved—but not in a roomful of hostile cops.

Sheila turned her head to avoid his gaze.

"Now that all the characters are assembled," Fiske announced dryly, "let's proceed. Detective Stankowsky, perhaps you'd like to start by explaining to Mr. Bollinger about recording this discussion and—"

"You can record anything you like," Max said quickly. "And I don't need a lawyer. I could have explained earlier, but I thought I could figure everything out for myself first."

"Figure what out?" Cowboy asked, leaning against the wall.

"The Furmire murder."

"So you admit you're involved."

"Not me. Not directly. But I knew someone in my family killed him."

"Why?"

Sheila sat down at the table and answered softly, "Because Max's father was into Furmire for a lot of money."

Her voice sounded empty—as though she were thinking about more than the conversation in the room. She had a faraway look in her eye, too; like a woman remembering many things—lost lovers, broken hearts, past mistakes. . . .

Max sat in the chair opposite hers. He longed to put his hands out to her, to hold her just for a second, but he refrained and spoke instead—to her, really. Only to her.

He said, "My father's life was made miserable by Enrique Furmire. Furmire had threatened him with everything—including the lives of his children and family. We all saw how my father suffered. I knew that one of us had decided to end it."

"By murdering a man?" Cowboy asked, his voice tinged with sarcasm.

"By murdering an animal," Max snapped, unable to check his temper. "Furmire used to send his goons around to beat up my father on a weekly basis. I happened to catch them at it one Friday night four years ago, so they beat me, too. I'm sure the hospital records will back up my story. The night Enrique Furmire disappeared, I was in the operating room at the city hospital."

Sheila questioned, "Where was your father?"

Max looked at her and found her eyes sharp again. "I'm not sure."

Cowboy asked, "Where was little Cameron?"

"Cameron was nineteen years old," Max replied. "Maybe he's never been terribly bright, but he'd never murder anybody. I doubt he'd ever be moved enough to commit anything but petty crime."

"Your mother?" asked Cowboy.

Max hesitated, damning his luck. If only he'd managed to find what he'd been looking for!

Sheila leaned forward. "Start from the beginning, Max. What have you figured out so far? You've been trying to solve the Furmire murder on your own, haven't you?"

"I didn't know it was a murder," Max pointed out. "I suspected it, but I only knew for certain that he'd disappeared. I'm almost certain my father did it."

"What makes you think so?"

Max took a breath. "Because he killed himself a few weeks later. He'd been despondent for a very short time. And he wouldn't have done something like that to himself for no particular reason, so I assumed he— Well, I assumed he became so distraught after killing a man that he couldn't live with himself. But I can't prove that. Not yet."

"What makes you think you can prove it?"

Max hadn't been able to talk to anyone about his father's death—not to his friends or his mother, not even to Cathy. He was amazed to find himself speaking calmly about a subject that had tormented him for four years—ever since the night he'd found his father hanging by an old length of harness from a beam in the brewery.

Max cleared his throat. "He must have left a letter. He wouldn't—he couldn't kill himself without explaining to me."

"And you think there's a suicide note somewhere in all his papers?"

"There's got to be."

All the cops looked at each other—Fiske, Cowboy, Sheila and the two uniformed cops who were standing by the window.

Sheila said, "There's stuff in file cabinets, in boxes—business paperwork all mixed up. Notebooks, ledgers, folders."

"We could send a team over," Cowboy suggested. "Three or four of us could do the job in no time."

Fiske said, "You going to sift through a bunch of file cabinets looking for a needle in a haystack?"

"It could explain a lot of things," Sheila responded. "It wouldn't hurt for us to take a look."

Testily, Fiske shot back. "Us? You just want to clear your boyfriend, Malone. Well, forget it. I want you off this case permanently. If anybody goes, it won't be you!"

Max spoke up: "Detective Malone has done her job all along. I'm the one who's made things difficult. I thought I would spare her a lot of trouble by keeping this to myself."

Fiske pointed his forefinger at Max's nose. "You shut up, buster, until you're spoken to, understand?"

Sheila didn't say anything. That's what scared Max the most. She sat in her chair, looking at a crack in the plaster. She was thinking—rolling something around in her head and trying to make some kind of decision. The blank expression on her face scared the hell out of Max.

Then Cowboy said, "Lieutenant, I think this guy is guilty. I bet I can prove it by shifting through all the paperwork back at his place. We can have the job done by morning."

Fiske nodded. "In the meantime, he can sit in detention. And Malone here can start typing."

Sheila got up from the table and left the room, not looking back. Max was handcuffed again and taken to the basement where he shared a poorly ventilated cell with a snoring drunk. Max wished he could make himself unconscious for a while, too. Inside, he was hurting. And this time the hurt wasn't just about his father.

Sheila typed her heart out.

It felt good, actually, to pound the keys on the old typewriter. She got rid of her hostilities while she mindlessly typed everything that had to do with the Furmire murder. While Cowboy took a couple of guys over to Max's loft, she thundered out a twelve-page report that was suitable for framing.

At ten o'clock that night—nine hours after Sheila started to work on the report—Cowboy staggered into the squad room.

Sheila got up from her desk and hurried to her obviously tired partner, even helping him off with his raincoat. "Well? What happened? Did you find anything?"

"Enough tax forms to float half the city. Man, I think I'm going blind after that ordeal!" He dug his knuckles into his bloodshot eyes. "Do you think I need glasses?"

"You need more help than glasses can give you. What else did you find, dammit? Tell me, Cowboy!"

He plopped into his chair, his head lolling backward in feigned exhaustion.

"What did you find?" Sheila demanded.

Her partner squinted open one eye to look at her. A grin played around his mouth. "A letter."

She eased down on the corner of his desk, unable to stand any longer. "What kind of letter?"

"A suicide letter, I'm pretty sure. Bollinger's old man confesses to the murder of Enrique Furmire, explains his motive and his feelings about having done the evil deed. There's some line about burying the body in the garden because it was the only place he figured it would never be disturbed. And then he wrote some sappy stuff to his son. Did you know Max found his dad's body?"

Sheila shook her head.

"Yep. Old man Bollinger hung himself from the rafters of the brewery. Pretty tough stuff. I guess Max has had some time to get over it."

Sheila thought about Max and his determination to get the Bollinger brewery going again. She shook her head. "I don't think he's over it yet."

Cowboy leaned back in his chair, closed his eyes again and sighed. "Anyway, we had to let Max go. It's pretty clear he had nothing to do with the murder, and we already know he's innocent in the Pletheridge break-in, so—"

"Where is he?"

Cowboy opened his eyes again, hearing the urgency in Sheila's voice. "Why do you want to know?"

"You know exactly why," Sheila snapped, getting to her feet.

"You're falling for the guy, aren't you?"

"For what it matters now, yes," Sheila admitted. "I fell hard for him."

"What do you mean, 'For what it matters now'?"

Sheila grabbed her jacket. "I think I've blown my chances of having a normal relationship with the man, don't you? How many lovers have you held at gunpoint?"

"And pulled the trigger."

"That was a warning shot."

Cowboy grinned. "Oh, he got the warning, all right. He wasn't going to budge an inch until you put that gun away. I think he was flabbergasted that it was loaded this time."

"Yeah," agreed Sheila. "Well, I've got a few things to explain to him, so I'm going downstairs."

"He's not there anymore."

"Where is he?"

Cowboy shrugged. "I dunno. He read the letter and seemed pretty broken up about it. He left. Maybe he went to check upon his little brother who's out on bail. Or maybe he went home."

Sheila put on her jacket and snapped off the lamp on her desk. She tossed the report at her partner. "Thanks, Cowboy."

"For what?"

"Looking for the letter. You did that tonight for me. You could have gone home for a hot dinner and some television with your wife, but you wanted to help me. I appreciate it."

Cowboy grinned. "You'd do the same for me."

Sheila laughed. "Maybe so."

"Hey, Malone?"

She turned in the doorway. "Yeah?"

"You're gonna be okay, I think," Cowboy said.

Sheila smiled. It was good to hear that from her partner.

She drove her car across the neighborhood and parked it in the alley between the brewery and Max's loft. Shutting off the engine, she sat in the car until the windows steamed up, thinking about what she could say to Max that would make everything good again. But she couldn't come up with anything that could do that.

So she screwed up her courage and went into the loft, deciding she was going to have to wing it.

Max wasn't there. Nor was he in the brewery.

Sheila couldn't think of a place where he might go to be alone, so she ended up driving to her apartment. Leaving the car parked in her aunt's backyard, she unlocked her door and went upstairs, tired, mentally worn-out and feeling more alone than she'd felt in a long time.

At the top of the stairs, she froze.

The sound of running water was coming from her bathroom.

With her heart skittering around under her ribs, she crept down the hall to the bathroom door. Light from the Victorian lamp over the mirror was casting a long golden glow into the hallway, and clouds of steam billowed in the air. Sheila put one shaky hand on the door and pushed it wider.

"Damn," said Max. "Where's your gun?"

He was in the shower—stark naked and looking very handsome. Sheila felt her knees wobble and she grabbed the door to stay upright. Water was puddling on the floor, and Max's clothes had been tossed across the sink. "What—what are you doing here?"

"What does it look like I'm doing?" His smile started slowly. "Want to join me?"

"Max, I—" Sheila's chest felt tight with fear, with longing, with a queer kind of release. On a quivering breath, she said, "Oh, Max."

"Come on," he said. "I knew you wanted to do it the first time. Take your clothes off."

She did, stripping off her sweater and jeans and kicking her boots into the hall. Sheila found she couldn't speak, and she was trembling so hard she had trouble with the snap on her bra. It came loose at last, and Max took her hand.

He pulled her under the spray, hugging her body against his slick, powerful frame. Against her ear he murmured, "Darling Sheila. I couldn't take the chance of not seeing you again. So I came here and waited."

"I looked for you, too. I went to your place."

"You did?" His laugh was soft and tense. "Why?"

"I didn't think you should be alone. Cowboy told me about the letter."

Max shook his head abruptly, as if shaking off a bad memory. "I knew it had to exist. I was glad to read it."

"I had to make sure you were okay. And—and I wanted to explain, to tell you—"

"There's nothing for you to explain. I know what you did and why you had to do it. I just wish I hadn't been such a fool in the brewery. I shouldn't have put you on the spot. The gun and— Well, I know how hard that was for you."

She hugged him tightly, pressing her face against his wet shoulder. The warm water streamed over their bodies. "I'm sorry, Max. I had to do what was right. I had to do my job."

"You play by the rules," he said. "I know that, and I'm glad."

"The system works. It gets screwed up sometimes, but it does work."

"When cops like you are doing the job, it works very well." Max smoothed a wet lock of her hair away from her cheek. "You're going to stick with it, aren't you?"

"What do you mean?"

"You're not going to finish law school. You were meant to be a cop, Sheila. And you proved you can do the job."

She relaxed her embrace and smiled a little. "Maybe so. But it won't hurt to finish school. I'll get too old for this job sooner or later. I only have a semester or two to go."

"A whole semester?" Max lifted her chin until he could look into her eyes. "You mean I can't have your complete attention for a whole semester?"

Sheila saw the fiery expression in his gaze and caught her breath. "Do you want my complete attention?"

He kissed her mouth warmly. "Every hour, every minute of it. I love you, Sheila Malone. I want to be with you always."

"Oh, Max. I love you, too." She wrapped her arms around his neck and reached up on tiptoe to touch his lips with hers.

With one hand, he pulled the flowered shower curtain closed. At once they were enveloped in steam and the rush of running water that teased every nerve-ending of Sheila's skin. Max's body felt hot and sleek against hers. His mouth was insistent, pressing her lips apart so that their tongues could play together. His hands slid lovingly down the wet curve of her back.

How quickly emotional love could turn to something far more erotic. A warm bubble of pleasure seemed to grow inside Sheila, spreading like liquid fire when it reached her loins.

Blindly she reached for the tube of herb-scented gel. Within half a minute, she filled her hands with sweet-smelling suds and began to lather Max's chest, his belly, his thighs, drawing patterns on his skin until he was thoroughly aroused. He swept a handful of the white foam off himself and with a gleam in his dark eyes, smoothed the lather across Sheila's shoulders and down to her breasts.

There was a catch in her voice as she whispered, "We should have done this the first time I caught you in the shower. Think how much trouble we could have avoided."

"But it wouldn't have been half so exciting."

She gasped as his soapy caress turned more intimate. "Speak for yourself, Slick."

He laughed deep in his throat. His palms and fingers traced every inch of Sheila's body, trailing lather from her earlobes to her chin, lingering at her nipples until she moaned, and caressing her belly as she writhed against him.

"I love you so much," he said, taking pains to rinse all the soap from her body and kissing each place to further excite her. "Sheila, you're so different."

"Maybe *we*'re too different."

"The hell with that," he muttered. "We'll celebrate the differences. They'll make us stronger. See how we fit together, Sheila."

She laughed unsteadily as he tried to find his way inside her body. "Not here," she gasped. "Let's go to my bed."

"Always by the rules." He sighed.

"Not *always*," Sheila said, and she proceeded to caress him with her mouth until Max laughingly cried for mercy and dragged her out of the streaming spray.

They grabbed towels, and Sheila ran for the bed. Half a step behind, Max followed and rolled her into the unmade bedclothes—both of them still wet and dizzy with pleasure. Max couldn't wait long enough to dry off. As their laughter died away, he sank inside her, and Sheila closed her eyes as they joined. It was different this time—more intense, perhaps; more joyful. Perfect.

Max murmured her name, and Sheila opened her eyes. She had never felt so complete as the moment their souls came together just then. Perhaps it was the same for him. They lay in awed silence, communing as one in a timeless embrace. Caressing the droplets from each other's skin with gentle fingertips, they held very still and breathed together. Then Max moved inside her. He was slow and languid with his first thrust, watching Sheila's face as she surrendered to her inner sensations.

She moved with him, too, knowing instinctively how to bring Max to the brink of ecstasy without letting him tumble over the edge. He groaned softly, all the while savoring her mouth, exploring the contours of her lips with his tongue. His hair felt coarse, but soft in her fingers, and his shoulders were warm and strong beneath her hands. Passion seemed to radiate from his skin. His body set hers afire.

At last an infinite and beautiful light seemed to grow inside her until the moment when they cried out as one and the light burned bright. Afterwards, Sheila spilled her heart to him, and Max said beautiful words in reply—words so intimate that she locked them away forever.

Later, Max dried her off with great care and tenderness, following each pat of the towel with a gentle kiss. Sheila lay in a haze of contentment, wondering if they had a chance—if it was possible for a tough Irish cop and an American aristocrat to have a life together. Was the love she felt brimming inside enough?

"We'll find a way to make this work," Max said softly, catching sight of the expression in her eyes.

"It won't be easy."

"I know. We've got a lot of things to talk about, a lot of things to set straight."

"Do you think it's possible, though? That we could have something good?"

"I think it's probable. Both of us are too stubborn to give up on something we really want. And I want you, Sheila. Very much. Now and forever, I want you to be my wife."

"You could be in for a lot of trouble," Sheila said with a grin as her concerns faded into nothingness.

"I'm counting on it," said Max, swooping down to kiss her once more.

*   *   *   *   *

Escape from it all
this summer with
Silhouette Summer Sizzlers

Three summer love stories from top
Silhouette authors in one special volume.

MISS GREENHORN	–	Diana Palmer
A BRIDGE TO DREAMS	–	Sherryl Woods
EASY COME . . .	–	Patricia Coughlin

Look out for Silhouette Summer Sizzlers from June 1991.
Priced £3.99.

Silhouette

Silhouette Desire

COMING NEXT MONTH

FOUR DOLLARS AND FIFTY-ONE CENTS
Lass Small

When her charity group decided to run a bachelor auction, Jan Folger was asked to approach her old playmate. She didn't anticipate that, when the local paper ran his picture, *every* woman in town would want to become his playmate!

PARADISE REMEMBERED
Carole Buck

For six years, Elyssa Collins had dreamed of a nameless, faceless stranger who aroused her deepest desires. She couldn't remember him, but she knew he was the father of her only child …

THE VALENTINE STREET HUSTLE
Ryanne Corey

Thomas Alexander Murphy was a loveable rogue; he dreamt of a tropical island paradise and he asked Michelle DeMara if she'd share his dream. Thomas was hard to resist, but she wanted a family, a home, responsibilities. How could they both have what they wanted?

COMING NEXT MONTH

HANDYMAN
Cathie Linz

Alicia Donnelly had sworn off struggling single
fathers looking for love, which was why when Mitch
Johnson belatedly announced the imminent arrival
of his young daughter, Alicia couldn't help feeling
betrayed. Did Mitch really want a baby-sitter or a
lover?

HEAT
Jean Barrett

Could Anne Richmond trust Ross McIntyre, the
brooding, dangerous American expatriate who was
her unwilling guide through the beautiful,
treacherous world of the upper reaches of the
Amazon?

NELSON'S BRAND
Diana Palmer

See how June's *Man of the Month*, Gene Nelson,
responds to a little tender loving care from Allison
Hathoway. This rugged rancher has his very own
brand of loving.